The White Witch

The White Witch

by Janet Graber

ROARING BROOK PRESS·NEW YORK

*Special thanks to Katherine Jacobs, an extraordinary
editor who asked the right questions and made the right
suggestions at the right time. I am grateful indeed.*

Published by Roaring Brook Press
175 Fifth Avenue
New York, New York 10010
www.roaringbrookpress.com

Roaring Brook Press is a division of
Holtzbrinck Publishing Holdings Limited Partnership
Text copyright © 2009 by Janet Graber
Distributed in Canada by H. B. Fenn and Company Ltd.

Cataloging-in-Publication Data is on file at the Library of Congress
ISBN-13: 978-1-59643-337-3
ISBN-10: 1-59643-337-X

Roaring Brook Press books are available for special promotions and premiums.
For details contact: Director of Special Markets, Holtzbrinck Publishers.

Book design by Scott Myles

First Edition May 2009
Printed in March 2009 in the United States of America
by RR Donnelley Company, Harrisonburg, Virginia

10 9 8 7 6 5 4 3 2 1

This book is dedicated to my darling Daddy.
I miss you now and forever.

1665 ◉ Church Register ◉ Parish of Letchlade

The Great Plague.
In it fifty died, after five hundred rooks
perched about the witch's cottage
till all five hundred died.
A great mysterie to see it.
A great wonder indeed.

chapter one

"What good fortune I happened upon a field of chamomile flowers this summer morn," I say, nipping the white-and-yellow blooms from their long, downy stalks. They flutter onto the scrubbed-wood table set beside the cottage door. "For a fomentation of chamomile will ease those swollen joints, Samuel, I promise you."

The old shepherd kneads his gnarled hands into a web of fingers and thumbs. "God bless you, Gwendoline Riston, for your healing ways. You've the gift, just like your poor departed ma."

Sad to say, my mammy died the day that I were born, but in truth Pappy has cared well for me these past fourteen years. I toss the flower heads into a jar, add two beakers of boiling water, and cover it tight to await the infusion.

"When does your pa return?" grunts Samuel, easing into Pappy's rocking chair beside the hearth.

"This very evening, if the fullness of the moon is my guide." Pappy is dear to me as all the world, and I miss him sore when he delivers wool from his barge to the merchants and weavers up and down the River Thames.

"Bringing word of that handsome rascal Jack Marlow, no doubt?"

I nod, but my heart lurches at the mention of Jack, apprenticed since early May to a wheelwright downriver in Oxford. He has been gone three long months, and I pray that Pappy has met up with him.

"Rest your weary limbs awhile, Samuel, and sup with us tonight," I say, straining the chamomile potion into a bottle. "Share in all Pappy's news."

"Thank you kindly, Gwendoline, but I must away." He struggles to push the medicine into the pocket of his smock. "For my dog tends the sheep alone on the common."

Samuel hobbles from the cottage, and I tick off my chores with haste. Eggs collected, speckled brown beauties piled in a bowl in the larder. Water pumped and in a pail beneath the table. Laundry hung upon the line. Pewter plates polished on the dresser. I tweak rosemary from a ceiling sprig and stir a pinch into the black cauldron of rabbit stew simmering over the fire.

Then snatching my cap, I dash down the lane past the smithy. The heat from the fire is near unbearable, but fat, fleshy Joe pumps away on his bellows and pounds the anvil just the same, sweat pouring from his dreary brow. A cheerless neighbor indeed.

As I hasten toward the village green, my skirt lifts in a sudden breeze.

"A scarlet frill sewn upon a petticoat," spits Mistress Mullin from her doorstep, "does naught but aid the Devil in his work."

She feeds a twisted hank of raw wool onto her spindle-whorl with nimble fingers and scowls at me. But then, she scowls at the world. Mistress Mullin still favors Oliver Cromwell's dull, drab ways, despite King Charles sits safe upon his throne and delights in ruffles and frills.

Over the green, past the tavern, through the churchyard, and across the meadow I fly to await Pappy's return. The scolding click of Mistress Mullin's spindle sticks fade into the sluggish air.

It is a fearsome hot summer. I toss aside my cap, kick off my wooden clogs, and sprawl beside the riverbank. It was a day much like this when Jack spilled into my life. Pappy had returned from a similar journey on the River Thames, with a filthy ragamuffin tucked beneath his cape. Under the grit and grime was a bonny boy with a thatch of auburn hair and freckles like a spray of pollen across his nose. *This lad will share our home, my angel here on earth girl*, Pappy had said, *for I could not leave him homeless and begging on the riverbank*. And we called him Jack, for he said it was his name, and Marlow because that is the town thirty miles west of London where Pappy discovered him.

I pull an apple from the pocket of my pinny and crunch my teeth into its rosy peel. A water vole, attracted by the sweet fruity smell, emerges from his bank house and wiggles his snout.

"Evening, little creature of God," I murmur, chewing steadily.

His ears twitch.

"Do you wish to sup?" I whisper.

He climbs into the palm of my hand and gnaws at the apple core with much grace. His whiskers wobble up and down. I stroke his chestnut brown fur. When his feasting is done, he dives into the river with a soft splash and disappears.

Mistress Mullin declares it witchy to commune with the animals and birds of the countryside. So be it. All God's creatures, I do declare.

The sun is set, and I gaze beyond the first looping bend in the meandering river where the ancient willow tree sweeps the surface of the water like a giant broom. No barge can I spy. I strain my ears for the distant sound of Rosie's harness bells but hear no telltale jingle-jangle. Where is Pappy? Has misfortune befallen him? But it is too soon to fret. A quibbling merchant must have caused Pappy delay. Or perhaps dear Rosie is simply slowed by the unusual summer heat.

How I hanker for Pappy's report of Jack and his new life in Oxford. Until Pappy rescued Jack and brought him home I had never possessed a playmate of my own. When my mammy died a white rook alighted on our chimney pot, an evil omen indeed according to Mistress Mullin. My fate was sealed when she peered into my cradle and spied my pale skin and thatch of ash white hair. A witchling was her verdict. And the villagers took notice nine months later when she birthed a daft babby. Ever after they and their children blamed me.

Jack was my one true friend. My trusty companion. Once when I tarried too long upon the wolds and was caught in a fearsome

gale, it was Jack came searching for me. His lantern flashed across
the hills. He found me taken shelter in one of Samuel's sheep-
folds, and there we stayed through all the night of lashing rain and
thunder and lightning, safe and dry beneath his cape.

Now the sweet little Ting-Tang bell, high in the church steeple,
tolls curfew across the meadow, warning all to be home in bed.
The moon is settled over the river, showering gleaming ripples,
like a myriad sparkling stars. Pushing stray curls under my cap,
I struggle into my clogs and toil back across the meadow and
through the churchyard of St. Giles.

Long ago, when Jack and I stole into the church to see for ourselves the damage that Puritan rule had wrought, we discovered
instead a secret chamber overflowing with paintings, silverware,
and pots of gold. Royalist riches Jack declared, hid well from Oliver
Cromwell and his parliament. It was our secret. Jack's and mine.

I slip swiftly into the shadows of the cottages down Sherborne
Lane. Something has roused the hens from their roosts, for they
scratch in their pens and set up an almighty squawking.

"Shame on you, Reynard," I chide, glimpsing a familiar bushy
tail. "Seek your supper in the woodland." And the wily dog fox
slinks away.

At home I open the door and an eerie shiver skitters across my
shoulder blades. I sense a presence in the darkened room. Has
Samuel returned after all to partake of my rabbit stew? But a rose
petal fragrance tells me it is Mistress Mullin's daughter, Hannah.
Many is the time I have glimpsed the older girl rinsing her long
black tresses with rose water when she thought herself alone. Her

gray skirt and weskit blend into the smudgy glow of the hearth.

"God's thunder, what are you doing here, Hannah?" I hold a spelk to the cinders and light the candle. "Did you not hear the curfew bell?" Her face is blotched with tears, her eyes swollen red, and snot drips from her nose. "Your brother Amos will be sent a-searching. If you are discovered with me, who your mother declares a witch, Lord knows what your punishment will be."

"I cannot worry on that now." Hannah shrugs. "Was your pa not due to return home this day?"

"What is it to do with you?" I snap.

"I must beg him take a message to Jack when next he journeys downriver. Our family will shortly board a ship bound for the New World," Hannah sobs, wringing a tear-sodden kerchief between slender fingers. "And I cannot bear the thought of it."

"But what has this to do with Jack?"

But even as I ask, I know what is true. My childhood companion long since sprouted to a handsome sapling, turning the heads of many an addle-brained lass about the village. Then Jack was not so much with me about my hearth. And I cannot forget the smarting hurtful sting I suffered when Jack chose Hannah Mullin to be Queen of the May. Not only that. Jack stole a kiss from Hannah as they twirled about the maypole. They are sweet on each other.

"I love Jack well," sighs Hannah. "We will wed."

"Wed!" I collapse onto the stool beside the hearth. "How can you wed?" My head throbs. "You must leave with your family to cross the sea."

Hannah kneels at my feet. "*Please* beg your pa give this to Jack."
She draws from her pocket the hair ribbon she wove through her
locks for the May Day dance, before she was dragged away by her
mother and beaten with a birch for flaunting such frippery. "Jack
will know then that I am in need of him."

"Jack is not free to drop all," I choke. "Pappy labored long to
seek this living for him. He is but sixteen and will be apprenticed
for years."

"We spoke before his leaving, Gwen. He swore naught would
keep him from me. If my family decided to risk the fearsome
ocean journey, I was to send a token."

My heart is a leaden weight in my chest; I so wished for Jack to
fetch me away over all the other village lassies. And now Hannah
Mullin dares to come here begging my help.

Brushing ashes from her skirt, Hannah rises from her knees.
"If need be, I will hide till Jack returns. My family will take their
passage without me."

"I doubt it, Hannah Mullin. Sorely I do."

Hannah dangles the token before me. "*Please* help me."

But I cannot move. My fingers clench. Hannah lets the shiny
yellow ribbon flutter into my lap, before slipping from the cottage, a silent ghostly shadow in the candle glow.

Envy gnaws at my gut, for now I know with certainty. Jack, whom
I love with all my heart, has pledged himself to Hannah Mullin.

chapter *two*

The skies are a vivid cornflower blue, the sun relentless, burning hotter day after day. Even the grass on the wolds singes brown. I tend my chores and wait daily on the riverbank for Pappy's return. And I avoid Hannah Mullin. For I do not wish to be reminded of her desire to wed Jack. 'Tis a foolish notion indeed since Jack is apprenticed and not free to marry.

On the seventh day of my riverbank vigil I am rewarded by the jingle-jangle of Rosie's harness bells long before she plods into view, for the river twists and turns for miles through the wide, flat pastures. I hasten down the rutted towpath, dodging piles of manure, waving my arms high in the air. So great is my excitement I knock my cap into the water and must fish it from the river with a long stiff teasel snapped from the bank.

"Greetings, Pappy!" I shout.

Pappy looms at the helm of his barge, the great hulking brawn of him, his long graying hair swept back in its pigtail beneath a floppy, felt hat.

"Evening, my angel here on earth girl."

I grab Rosie's bridle and bury my face into her thick mane, breathing in her wondrous oaty breath.

"What kept you, Pappy?" I call.

His face darkens as a thundercloud. "Hush with any questions, Gwen-child," says Pappy. "Help me secure the barge." He throws the pulling ropes onto the riverbank, and I coil them into neat piles, before unhitching the swingle-tree from beneath Rosie's tail.

I lead Rosie through the meadow, and Pappy limps along behind. His leg was near sliced in two by a sword during the Civil War between Cromwell's Roundheads and the King's Cavaliers. It was luck no surgeon got hold of him, he's fond of saying, or he'd of lost the leg altogether. According to Pap 'twas my mammy who nursed him back to health with the aid of the self-heal plant and juice from the common field poppy.

When we reach the pump Pappy rolls up his sleeves and sluices water onto his face and neck and arms. Finally, he finds his tongue. "Call out our neighbors, Gwen-child. Be quick about it." His lips are drawn in a line as straight as an old Roman road.

"Can it not wait, Pappy? Supper simmers—"

"Gwendoline," he snaps. "Do as you are bid!"

I know better than to ask another question. I thump on doors, lean over front steps, shout through open windows, as I am told.

And soon all fifty-five inhabitants of Letchlade cluster about the trough. All but Hannah. I know not what she is about since our conversation a week past, and I care little.

I pump the trough full and Rosie slurps the good, clear water. She has had a long journey of it pulling the barge along the towpaths in the stifling summer heat. Bothersome bluebottles buzz about her head.

"What's on your mind, Robert Riston?" asks Samuel, stooped over his shepherd's crook. Yet his knuckles are less swollen, I am pleased to see. The collie dog sidles up in search of a comfort. I stroke his narrow muzzle and slip him a morsel of dried venison.

"A sickness in London. The Great Plague, they call it." Pappy leans upon the trough to ease his aching leg. "King Charles has removed his court to Isleworth."

"Good riddance to bad rubbish," remarks Mistress Mullin. "Let him remove himself farther still!"

"What business is it to us?" demands Mistress Bramwell.

"Serious business!" shouts Pappy. "People drop like leaves from the trees in autumn. It is a terrible ordeal. Chills. Fevers. Fearsome head pains."

"We all suffer the ague one time or another," Old Samuel says, nodding. "But you may well be right this is something more."

"Indeed, it is more, Samuel," Pappy presses on. "Swellings in the neck, armpit, and groin. Purple-black blotches under the skin. Almost always the good Lord calls his sufferers home."

I shudder. There is a silence about the village green. Dread hangs in the stifling hot air, sharp and sour.

"Listen!" bellows Pappy. "It is the talk of the river. I could scarce complete my task for folks pouring out of London on foot and by barge. Seeking sanctuary where they may."

"Well I for one have no time for idle gossip," mutters Mistress Mullin. "The good Lord will save those he sees fit." One by one folks make to slink away from Pappy's voice of doom.

"Pay heed!" Pappy's face flames red with anger. "This sickness travels with much speed. It spreads fast, you mark my words."

"Why should we listen to you, Robert Riston?" grumbles Joe from the smithy. "I for one heed you not. Your witchy wife delivered my wench a dead babby." Joe's fleshy jowls wobble with ancient misery. "Then let her die of it."

"Aye. But many more babbies did she save," argues Old Samuel. "And well you know it." He whistles the dog to his side and shuffles off in disgust.

"Please hear me," begs Pappy.

"We're a hundred-odd miles from London by water," scoffs Joe. "That's safe enough, in my opinion."

"'Tis not," argues Pappy. "I have seen with my own eyes. Evacuees will soon arrive. We must close off the village. Barricade the roads. Let no bargemen set foot in the meadow."

"Gracious sakes, Robert, we can't do that," laughs Mistress Goody. "What a notion. Master Goody will make a gift to the Church of St. Giles. That will keep us safe. Buy us peace of mind!"

The entire village turns its back on Pappy. The womenfolk head back to their hearths and cooking pots, the menfolk to the tavern for false succor.

"Come, Gwen-child." Pappy sighs. "We will make our own plan, and be quick about it."

I stable Rosie in the barn behind our cottage. I brush her black coat free of mud splashes and burrs and scoop fresh oats into a bucket.

In the cottage I serve Pappy a platter of mutton stew with a loaf of fresh-baked bread and a beaker of ale.

"What must we to do, Pappy?"

He chews his meat steadily but says naught. A log lurches in the hearth and sparks shoot up the chimney.

"Perhaps the illness will wear itself out before it can travel upstream to Letchlade?" I say.

"Nay, I fear that is not so, child. I fear it greatly."

"I do not wish to die," I whisper.

Pappy pushes aside his plate and begins to pace. His gammy leg drags behind him, scraping and scuffling on the stone floor.

I dip Pappy's gravy-stained platter into a tub of water. "Perhaps *I* know what we might do," I murmur.

"Then tell me, Gwen-child."

"There is a concealed chamber above the porch of St. Giles. Could we not hide ourselves there, away from the pestilence?" I rub the platter dry on a piece of sackcloth and place it back upon the dresser.

Pappy stops his rasping tread to gawk at me and rakes his weatherworn hands through his long, graying hair. "But how in God's thunder do you know of this place?"

If I am to be punished for keeping this secret, I do not care. Not if it will save our lives. "During the rule of Cromwell, Jack and

I sneaked into St. Giles to see for ourselves what damage was done
by the Roundheads. I tripped on an uneven flagstone and tumbled
against the wall. A slab of stone grated and grazed and fell inward.
Jack and I discovered secret stairs leading to a secret chamber. We
played Hideaway there upon occasion."

"Played Hideaway!" His blue eyes flash in the candlelight.

I think I will surely be punished, but instead Pappy bursts into
gales of laughter and collapses into his rocking chair beside the
open hearth.

"And what was in this chamber," he chuckles, "where you and
Jack played your Hideaway games?"

"Paintings. Tapestries. Communion plate. Silver and gold," I
stammer. "But we touched it not." I cross my fingers in the folds
of my skirt. It is only a fib, after all. For we always left the riches as
we found them.

"I believe you, Gwen-child," he chuckles again. "You stumbled
on my Royalist hideout where I hid Lord Bathurst's treasure trove
all through the Civil War and gave it back when the monarchy
was restored."

"Your hideout!"

"In a manner of speaking. That room provided safe haven
for more than one Cavalier on the run, not least of all King
Charles himself."

I can scarce believe it. Pappy hid fugitives there, including
King Charles I. Sadly, was all for naught for the King lost his
head when the war ended.

"When Cromwell's men tried to torch the Manor House at

the end of the war," Pappy continues, "I risked life and limb to rescue Lady Bathurst. The poor woman was with child. Your ma did tend her needs, and we concealed her in the secret chamber for several nights until she could be carried down-river to safety."

Never has he said a word. Prideful, he most certain is not.

"I know not how I forgot this place, Gwen-child, except to say I am so a-feared of losing you I could think of naught at all. But now we must waste no time in making use of this secret chamber yet again!" Pappy rises to his feet. "The infected will soon arrive. Your only hope of survival is to avoid contact with them."

"And yours, Pappy." Then a great wash of fear grips me. "Wait! What of Jack? We must keep Jack safe, too."

Pappy seeks my hand. "Gwen-child, I am greatly worried for our Jack. I had arranged to meet him under Osney Bridge." The candle upon the table sputters; whirls of wax drip into its saucer. "I waited in vain."

"But why did you not visit Jack where he is apprenticed?" I choke. It is unlike Pappy to bide his time and wait for anything.

"Oxford is greatly afraid of the Plague. The city Fathers forbade us from our boats. But now I must venture downriver again as fast as possible to discover what has become of Jack, for I love him as my own son."

My heart weighs heavy in my chest. How I yearn to hear the rumble of Jack's voice and the thump of his boots about the cottage. "But you say that Oxford is barricaded against travelers."

"This time I shall find a way into the city to seek Jack, and we will take refuge on the barge till this suffering passes."

"Take me with you," I plead. "For I love Jack, too."

"Nay, child. You must be concealed in the secret chamber this very night, safe and secure from this monstrous misery abroad in the land."

chapter three

"Pappy, do not leave me," I beg. "Do not lock me away from the birds of the sky and the creatures of the wolds by myself. I can bear it not."

"Halt your blather, child. For we must make haste." Pappy limps into the larder and slings provisions into a burlap sack.

"The chamber will be your only home," he pants. "Your retreat. You must not leave it. Not even to pump water." He flings flagons of ale and cider about his neck. "Be sparing with these. I cannot judge how long they must last."

I am struck dumb at his terrible speed. Rosie needs rest. Who will scatter grain for my chickens? Tend my garden? My mind swirls like the river in flood. Are all these things to be lost to me?

"Collect your belongings," Pappy orders.

I hasten up the ladder to my attic room. On the sill is the toy
bird Pappy carved me from sun-bleached wood. Never did he
grow weary of recounting the day of my birth, when the white rook
flew from the spinney of trees to perch upon our chimney. *'Twas
your mammy's guardian angel, Gwen-child, come to carry her soul to
heaven.* Pappy's version does trump that of Mistress Mullin, who
lost no time declaring the bird to be the Devil in disguise.

From the cupboard I remove my cloak, three wool skirts, a
shawl, four linen shifts, three blouses, and a bodice, all of which
I tuck into a sturdy leather satchel. On the floor beside my bed
lay the kingfisher blue hose I am struggling to knit for Jack. I am
not neat and quick with my fingers like the other village lassies,
but the coming days will be long. With a sigh I add the needles
and yarn to the bag along with my precious wooden bird. Down-
stairs I gather up the chamber pot, as well as a sharp knife, plate,
and beaker.

"Hurry, Gwen-child," says Pappy. "Ting-Tang has rung."

I gaze about our herb-scented room. The bed in the corner
where I was born and where my mammy died. Pewter platters
sparkle on the dresser. Pappy's empty rocking chair sits beside
the hearth.

But from the corner of my eye, in the darkest recess behind the
settle, I spy Hannah Mullin's bright yellow hair ribbon. I try not
to see it. I try to forget that I thrust it there.

"Come, Gwendoline, time is a-wasting," calls Pappy from
the door. Along with the provisions, he has slung a sheaf of new
mown hay over his shoulder.

"Yes, Pappy." Cinders tumble in the hearth. Shadows leap on the walls. Swiftly I pluck the yellow ribbon from its hideaway, before blowing out the candle.

We creep down the lane under a starlit sky. The heat is still oppressive, with not a sign of rain. My skirt drags in the dry earth. Pappy's gammy leg dredges through the dirt. When we slip past the Mullin cottage a voice rises in anger, followed by a sharp slap. Hannah's ribbon tingles in my apron pocket.

Up the path of St. Giles Church we lug our bundles. Pappy pushes open the iron-studded door of the porch. I rest for a moment on the stone bench, gouged deep with scars where Roundhead soldiers sharpened their blades during the time of the Civil War.

Pappy cups my cheeks in his hands. "It must be done, Gwen-child. The secret chamber will keep you alive as it has many others in the past, for you are special indeed. Blessed with a gift of healing."

"Not a witch then, despite Mistress Mullin's declarations?"

Pappy lifts my cap and runs his thick fingers through my ivory tresses. "Pay her no heed," he says, spreading my hair about my shoulders. "'Tis all because you resemble an angle abiding here on earth, just as did your poor departed ma."

I smile for Pappy. But it is not easy to be shunned on account of my appearance. To be sure there are many more peculiar than me.

Pappy hefts the sheaf of hay over his shoulder, along with the flagons of ale and the bulging burlap sack. I gather up my leather bag and we enter the silent church. Moonlight streams through the clerestory windows high above the nave. Candles flicker on the altar. A rich aroma of tallow fat mingles with ancient dust. I dip my fingers in the holy water and bow to the wood-carved Madonna.

Pappy goes direct to the secret slab and presses his palm firmly on the stone. It creaks and grinds and opens inward to the secret stairway. I follow him up the narrow twisting stone steps to the small wood door.

"The secret chamber of Gwendoline Riston," he sighs, stepping into the modest room. "It must suffice indeed."

Dust lies thick upon the floor, and dead flies smatter the windowsill. Cobwebs hang from the narrow latticed window like tatted lace. The tiny diamond panes are a patchwork of plain glass and milk glass, which I trust will camouflage me well from any nosy neighbors. I unlatch the casement.

"Use caution in the daytime, Gwen-child," warns Pappy. "But methinks it safe enough to open the window after curfew, when all are a-bed."

I squeeze my head and shoulders through the window and gulp the night air. One way affords me a clear view across the meadow to the river. The other looks directly onto the village green and beyond to our own thatched cottage at the end of Sherborne Lane. In deep shadow I spy Rosie's barn and the dense spinney of trees. Already I miss it all sore.

"Gwendoline's chamber." Pappy kisses my forehead. "Stay within. No matter what happens. No matter what you see. No matter what you hear. Stay. For I cannot lose you, my angel here on earth girl, truly I cannot."

"Then take me with you, Pappy," I implore once again. "Do not leave me here alone."

Pappy shakes his head, and the pigtail thumps back and forth. "Here you will be safe from the plague." His voice sounds far away. As if he has already departed upon his journey back to Oxford. "For I am certain sure the contagion is passed one person to another in some odd way that I cannot fathom. Naught will stop its passage till it has run its course."

My body shakes head to foot. "What if you do not find Jack?" I cry. "What if you catch the sickness? What if you die? What happens to me then?"

"You are a brave lass, Gwendoline. If necessary, make haste to seek Lord Bathurst when you deem the plague has passed."

"Where in heaven's name am I to find his Lordship?" I sob.

"He lingers now with the King's entourage in Isleworth. But I hear they will shortly move upriver to Hampton Court, the better to avoid the sickness." Pappy pulls me to his chest and I breathe the familiar odor of fresh-sheared fleece mingled with damp river pastures. "Lord Bathurst will not forget his debt to me," he murmurs. "Find him. Beg his protection. For I fear there are some who will be quick to lay blame at your door."

Pappy blinks and kisses me quick. Then he's gone. My dearest Pap, who does put others before himself at every turn, limps down the churchyard path toward Sherborne Lane. A short time later he leads Rosie from her barn and clops through the meadow toward the river. I wave from the shadows until the

faint muffle of Rosie's hooves ceases. But Pappy does not turn
his head, nor slow his tread, lest he expose my hideaway.

An unbearable sadness descends upon me. I observe my
hideaway by the light of the moon hanging like a beacon in the
sky. To keep from weeping the night away, I set about arranging
my chamber. I remove the dust and dead flies best I can with
a broom fashioned from a swatch of hay. The task is long and
tedious, but I brood not, for what will I do when my housekeep-
ing is complete?

The chest is bare. When Jack and I first peeked, it bore a
quantity of sacks containing gold coins. On many a dark winter
day we sneaked away to play King and Queen. Jack perched upon
the stool as if it were his throne and issued orders to his serfs. I
swathed myself in tapestry and tossed coins hither and thither
like a bountiful queen.

Tonight I fold all my clothing, except my cloak, inside the
chest. My precious toy bird and the half-knitted hose I set upon
the windowsill. The knife and plate and beaker I place on the
stool. The chamber pot fits nicely beneath.

I stack the provisions on a low stone shelf: six loaves of
bread; a wheel of cheese; a smoked eel of goodly size; three
dozen strips of dried venison; an abundance of parsnip,
carrots, and turnip; and early autumn apples. To quench my
thirst I have four large flagons of ale, three of cider. On a
whim I take up the knife to nick a mark on the wall beneath
the sill. But surely I shall be free of this place long before my
supply is eaten?

I stuff the empty sack tight with the remains of the fresh hay, heave my new mattress upon the chest, and cover it with my woolen cloak. Weary beyond measure I close the window and kneel before the crucifix nailed to the plastered wall. Did the doomed King Charles place it here, or perhaps Lady Bathurst, whilst Pappy kept her hid from the Roundheads?

When at last I lay down, I toss and turn till a din explodes about me so raucous I fear I am transported to Bedlam. But it is only Master Matty ringing the belfry bells that hang beneath sweet Ting-Tang. I stumble from my mattress of hay and clasp my ears till he is done calling everyone to Sunday prayer.

The sky is deeply mauve, streaked with ribbons of cloud. But there is still no sign of rain to relieve the long drought. Despite Pappy's concern, I open my window a crack so that I may catch what is said in the village below and for a breath of fresh air. The chamber is stifling hot.

One by one my neighbors progress up the churchyard path, even the Mullin family, despite their vocal disputes with our vicar the Reverend Thomas Morton over the return of incense, candles, and altar clothes to our church. Popish nonsense, declares Mistress Mullin at every opportunity.

Fifteen-year-old Hannah treads soft behind her oafish brothers. Amos is seventeen and burly built like his pa, with broad shoulders and bulging thighs. But poor Noah, nine months younger than me, is squat, flat-faced, and dense. He forever stumps along behind his older brother on bandy legs without a single thought in his head. And I am blamed for his plight.

I spy a bruise upon Hannah's cheek. She was ill used yet again last evening. My fingers crumple her yellow ribbon still lying in my pocket. I am sure Pappy would gladly have delivered it to Jack. But envy bores through me like weevils in a sack of flour. What I hope for most in all this world is that Hannah must travel with her family far away over the vast ocean.

chapter *four*

I wear naught but a blouse and my frilled petticoat, for a heavy heat hangs over Letchlade as thick and oppressive as a wet wool fleece. When matins is over, I slice a piece of dried eel for my noonday meal and wash it down with a beaker of ale, before falling into a fitful slumber. The rumble of a cart soon wakes me. I know the squeak and squeal of Joe's wagon wheels in our lane. I know the screech of the dray fetching ale to the White Hart Tavern. But this odd racket approaches from the Cirencester road and is strange to my ears. I crouch beneath the sill and peer through the window to discover what is happening.

A peddler shields his eyes to scan the cottages, which sparkle like meadow cowslips in the glare of the yellow sun. He reins in his nag upon the green. She dips her nose into the trough and gulps gratefully. What a sorry excuse for a horse. Mangy coat, protruding ribs, and an open sore that begs a warm poultice of flaxseed oil.

The driver leaps from his cart and lopes door to door, much as I did only yesterday. Already it seems a very long time ago. His black cloak streams behind him and he looks for all the world like the angel of death.

"Come out, good folks," he hollers. "Gather round."

Dust rises in the lanes like curls of smoke as neighbors shuffle into view.

"What business do you have with us?" shouts Mistress Goody, stomping across the green. "Do you not know it is the Sabbath day?"

"The sickness makes no mind of the Sabbath," he retorts. "The plague is fast approaching." He busies himself opening baskets and boxes, and setting out trinkets on the back of his cart. "Buy my wares," he calls. "Sapphires, ambers, emeralds, amethysts." I doubt the baubles are what he claims, for they shimmer not, but resemble more pebbles plucked from the river. "Powders, pills, potions." He shakes jars into the air. "Meat of adder, skin of toad, juice of a garden snail. Any or all will protect you well!"

"My family is saved already," gloats Mistress Goody. "Master Goody made a gift to St. Giles Church this very day. Be on your way."

But he takes not the slightest notice. In no time the peddler is rewarded with eager customers pushing and shoving around the cart for a better view of his gimcracks. All except Hannah, who shuns the crowd. She is hunched on her front doorstep, scuffing her clogs through the dirt, quietly watching.

When Samuel's dog sniffs the stranger's heels, he is rewarded with a swift kick. The collie yelps in pain. I bite my lip so as not to cry out at this cruelty.

"You need be rid of any dogs," advises the peddler. "They do carry the disease fast as an east wind."

"Robert Riston did warn of the plague just yesterday. He did not mention dogs in all his rambling," sniffs Mistress Bramwell.

"Aye, and today Robert Riston is gone," informs Joe from the smithy, huffing and puffing up Sherborne Lane on his fat flat feet.

"Gone?" mutters Mistress Mullin.

"The Riston cottage is boarded up." Joe gasps for breath. "The horse is gone. And there's not a sign of the pale one."

"She could lurk anywhere," snaps Mistress Mullin. "Gwendoline Riston is a witch, just like her ma. You all saw her familiar and how it did hex my belly. That is proof enough of the Devil's work. If sickness comes to Letchlade it will be her doing, mark my words."

Fear oozes out of my every pore. In the blink of an eye Mistress Mullin has tossed blame my way. She always has. May God and this chamber protect me from her vindictive ways.

"Purchase a remedy," shrieks the angel of death. "Eye of newt. Claw of cat. All will safeguard you from disease *and* witchery." He hastens amongst the anxious villagers in his glossy black cloak pushing his wares. Now he reminds me of a busy beetle scurrying from rock to rock in anticipation of a coming storm.

I hear the porch door beneath me open, and then Reverend

Morton strides down the path between the gravestones clutching a golden crucifix. He hurtles into the throng surrounding the peddler, his face mottled crimson with anger. "When quacks appear with worthless talismans, death can not be far removed," he tells his congregation. "There is only one savior, and that is Christ our Lord. Get upon your knees, all of you, and pray to the Lord for mercy."

He makes the sign of the cross over and over again, as if this very gesture will cause his parishioners to obey. But he might as well be invisible. They thrust hard-earned groats into the grasping fingers of the peddler as fast as they can and scoop up his charms to ward off the plague as well as witchy spells.

All the while Hannah waits in the shadows.

For what, I wonder? The coming plague? Her family's departure to the New World? For Pappy to deliver her token to Jack? And then it comes to me that what Hannah Mullin does is wait patiently for Jack Marlow. My Jack.

Suddenly a terrible hubbub distracts us all. The sky is so dark that for several moments I think a long awaited storm is approaching. An eerie whirring fills the air. Much like a swarm of angry bees. The crowd, still bunched around the peddler's cart, cast fearful eyes skyward, clasping their newly purchased talismans to their chests.

But it is a flock of birds flown from the spinney of trees behind my cottage. A furious black cloud of rooks is wheeling and spinning in the heavens above. It is so large not a speck of blue sky can I see through my windowpanes.

"What did I tell you!" I hear Mistress Mullin shriek.

The rooks scream and squawk as loud as the bells this very morning.

"There's no surer sign of witchy work than a flock of rooks. The pale one casts a spell." Mistress Mullin's words hurtle through my window like poisoned arrows.

Abruptly, the huge black birds bank high over the crowd and whirl down Sherborne Lane back toward their rookery. Instead of coming to rest in the elms they roost upon the roof of my cottage, in my garden, and upon Rosie's barn, a sullen bevy of big black birds.

"Mistress Mullin speaks the truth," Joe shouts. "The pale one has used the birds to cast a spell upon us." His thick black hair, lank with sweat, sticks in clumps to his ruddy cheeks.

"Like that rook on her roof gave Ma the evil eye," brays Amos Mullin, clomping over the green.

"White rook," jabbers Noah Mullin, thumping after Amos.

"What more proof do we need?" Joe waves his blistered fists in the air. "Let's get rid of the birds and break the pale one's spell once and for all."

Despite the fearful heat, I shiver and shake. Goose bumps bloom on my bare arms. What on earth does Joe plan to do? The rooks roost quietly now causing no harm, but I fear they are doomed.

The peddler has had enough. He packs up his wares, leaps back upon the seat of his cart, and urges the poor nag away from the rooks, away from the green, and out onto the open road.

It seems Hannah too has had enough of this madness. She slips silent as a ghost behind her cottage and takes refuge in her cow barn. But the rest of the villagers scramble to collect pots and pans from their hearths, sticks from the woods, stones from the ditches, and follow Joe and the lame-brained Mullin brothers. The crowd surges forward, banging and clanging their tools down Sherborne Lane. They hesitate and then move again. The mob surrounds my dwelling, making a fearsome racket.

The birds stay still as statues.

The mob rattle their sticks and hurl their stones.

What manner of birds are these that nothing will budge them from their perches? Fly away birds. Please fly away. Please, God, let them not be harmed.

Now smoke pours forth from the forge. Joe's bellows pump away. Moments later he emerges with a flaming torch clutched in his fist. He hurls his torch upon the thatched roof of my cottage. The tinder-dry straw catches. Sparks sizzle and scurry along the eaves. Flames lick down the walls and whip around the door.

But the rooks in the garden and the rooks upon Rosie's barn swarm to join the rooks upon my roof.

"Go! Fly away!" I cry. "Else you will die."

The birds perch, still as stone, like dead men shrouded in black robes.

"Be gone!" I beg. "Leave now." But the birds heed me not.

Timbers crackle and crumble. Flames billow into the sky. And my home explodes in an inferno of fire, taking with it each and every sleek black rook.

I am in such a tremble I collapse upon my bed. One thing is crystal clear. No one will believe now that I am not a witch.

chapter *five*

The charred smell of smoldering timbers and burnt rook hovered over Letchlade for days afterward. Now all that remains of my home is the stone chimney piece, a bleak blackened monument. I can scarce believe Joe did such a cruel and terrible thing. Despite he blames my mammy for the loss of his wife and babby, how can he truly believe that burning down our cottage will keep the plague from the village?

Each day of my seclusion passes slow as a snail upon a blade of meadow grass. And I ponder now if Pappy did misjudge the spread of the disease, for below my secret chamber life in Letchlade continues on much as before—menfolk tend crops in the fields; womenfolk spin and weave upon their doorsteps; lads and lassies frolic upon the green.

I find ways to fill my time, lest I be driven mad, for already there are twenty scratches upon my wall. I pace the chamber daily, taking as many strides as is needed to reach the river, so that I do not lose the use of my limbs.

Each day I try to recall at least one herb or plant or bark or berry that hung from the rafters of my cottage—*field poppy milk to ease pain; hedgerow lady's straw to curdle milk for cheese; hound's tongue root to bind; fleabane for gut ache; starry stitchwort for an aching side*—so my mind does not become befuddled.

On this twentieth night of my isolation I lie upon my mattress in a misery, plucking idly at the scarlet frill on my petticoat. If I do not take care, the stitching will unravel and I will have naught to cheer me in this dreary place.

Suddenly I hear soft footsteps treading up the stairs leading to my chamber. Fear takes hold, so I can hardly breathe. I hasten to the table to grasp my knife. I will not go easily. The door gnaws slowly across the stone floor. A shape stands in the doorway. I lunge.

"No!" Fingers clasp my wrist, and the knife clatters to the floor. And by the light of the full moon I find myself face-to-face with Hannah Mullin.

"By all that is holy, what brings you here?" I gasp, shaking free of her grasp. My head aches with bad ale and the shock of discovery.

Hannah's eyes glisten in the moonlight.

"How do you know of this place? No one knows of my chamber but Pappy." I bite my lip to stifle a cry of fury. "And Jack."

Again I know the truth. Jack has shared *our* secret with Hannah. Not even this could he keep for *me*. My mind spins. Jack has betrayed me. Hannah, the daughter of Mistress Mullin, knows of my hideaway. I am utterly alone and in grave danger.

"My family leaves within days for their voyage to the New World," Hannah gulps. "For the love of God, let me hide with you."

"What!" I gaze at her, startled. She wants to stay in my chamber where Pappy bade me meet with no one. Where I am driven mad with worry for his safety and that of Jack. Now this wretched girl, who has stolen Jack's heart, wants to join me.

"If I come on the eve of their departure," Hannah says, "it will be too late for my family to tarry, for the ship will not wait. When Jack receives my token he will seek me here."

The yellow hair ribbon lies uneasy in my pinny pocket. My palms are cold and clammy with the knowledge of my deception.

"Here? Jack will look for you here?" My brain is so befuddled by her scheme that I cannot think straight.

"Jack showed me how to gain entrance. So that if the need arose I could take refuge."

"You think of naught but yourself," I cry.

Hannah takes a step toward me. "Nay, Gwendoline, 'tis not so. But I cannot allow myself to be taken across the world to dress in drab my whole life, to never sing or dance or make merry, to marry someone I love not—"

"But you cannot marry Jack. It is not fair, it's—"

"Oh, you poor lass. " Hannah clutches her hand to her mouth. "Can it be that you also hanker for Jack?"

"No!" A flush creeps up my neck and onto my cheeks. "No,

of course not." Never will I confide in this girl that I craved for
Jack to fetch me away and crown me Queen of the May.

"I have no wish to hurt you, Gwendoline," Hannah murmurs.
"Truly I have not."

I slump upon my bed in a daze. My leaden heart weighs heavy
as ever in my chest. I suppose I always believed Jack would come
back to Pappy and me when his apprenticeship ended, foolish girl
that I am.

"Jack promised to gain me a position as maidservant in his
master's household. And when Jack has learned well his trade we
can wed, and—"

She rambles on till my head swirls like maypole ribbons. None
of this did Jack confide to Pappy or me. How could he have been
so selfish?

"Did your pa go downriver to seek Jack?"

I nod. "It is fear of the plague that makes Pappy keep me here.
I promised not to venture forth, promised to have contact with no
one. I must obey. Besides, if your ma discovers me she will see me
roasted like the rooks."

Tears pour down my cheeks: for the lost birds, my lost home,
not being fetched away. My arms gleam ghostly white in the dreary
room and suddenly I am seized with despair.

"Do you believe me a witch, like your ma?" I sob.

"Of course not, Gwendoline. It is silly nonsense." Hannah
settles beside me on the mattress and I let her. "I never thought it
right that she brand you so and sway all in our village against you."
But when Hannah reaches out to smooth my hair I jerk away.

"Ma's a-feared of you, lass, with your silver-white curls and mist gray eyes. She's a-feared that if you can heal, you can just as easily harm. But in my mind it is all prattle."

I gaze at Hannah, whose fate rests in my hands. If I refuse her refuge she will be removed to another land, far from Jack, just as I desire. But if Jack returns, how will I face him when he learns I did naught to save the lassie he loves?

"Come when you must," I mutter.

Next morning I discover Hannah has delivered to my door a pail of fresh water, as well as a small square of tallow soap and a wooden comb.

I pull the comb through my hair before casting off my scarlet-trimmed petticoat to bathe my body head to toe. What joy to rid myself of sweat and grime. I can think of naught more advantageous and pleasant than to smell sweet, though it is considered by most folks harmful to cleanse the body often. Once Hannah's ma caught me frolicking in the river, sleek and shiny as an otter, and near burst in two like a ripe plum declaring this sport to be witchy indeed!

When I am done bathing, I swish my soiled garments in the bucket and spread them upon the stone floor to dry. I try to imagine sharing this small chamber with Hannah. It will be hard indeed to hide my jealous nature from her in such a confined space. But I must find a way to accept her rather than let this envy fester in my soul. How I will accomplish this I cannot say.

I rest my elbows on the sill and peer out of my window. The day
promises to be hot once again, with no hint of rain clouds forming
upon the wolds. I turn my gaze to the river, and my heart plunges
clear to my sparkling clean toes. For what I observe is a large London barge preparing to dock. So Pappy *was* right to predict a flood
of refugees fleeing London. Have they passed Pappy's boat on the
river? Perhaps given news of the plague? Might they be sickening
of it themselves, but not yet know it? It is just as Pappy feared.

I nibble on a carrot and watch the travelers disembark from
the vessel, hauling quantities of trappings onto the riverbank
including kegs of beer and sacks of grain. There is much hulla-
balooing and pushing and shoving as some forty or so newcomers trek across the meadow. Three families are dressed in much
finery, the men sporting velvet breeches and frill-cuffed coats,
the women wearing gowns of satin and lace. They go directly to
the inn, accompanied by servants pushing handcarts of luggage.

The poor folks, many clutching babbies, drag their meager
belongings in coarse canvas sacks and willow baskets onto the
village green. They swill mouthfuls of water at the trough and
splash sweat from their weary faces. Those with groats to pay gain
refuge by cottage hearths. The rest no doubt will sleep in barns
or under haystacks.

As the day wears on, Mistress Goody does not hesitate to take
advantage of these strangers. By noon her window ledge is arrayed
with meat pies, pasties, and cottage loaves in great abundance.
I am glued to my casement for my mouth waters and my stomach
cramps for just one mouthful of home-baked bread soaked in

milk fresh from the udder. How tired I am of naught but dried
meat and withered vegetables washed down with warm ale.

A skinny ragamuffin with a tangle of ginger hair catches my
eye. His spindly legs are covered in sores and he appears to belong
to no one. My lips twitch into a smile when I observe the little
tyke deftly sidle around Mistress Goody's ample hips and snatch
a pasty from her sill. He darts up Dykes Lane toward the grazing
common where no doubt he can fill his stomach in peace.

When night finally falls the gentry make no mind of our
curfew bell. Fueled with quantities of spirit, they dance about in
giddy circles on the village green to the accompaniment of drum
and pipes. Twirling plumed three-cornered hats and waving
feathered fans, they gambol without a care in the world.

Since they are all too addled to notice, I throw open my
window and look to the London barge from whence they came.
It bobs gently on the river, lit by a great round moon. And
then, in the shadows, I notice an abundance of gray-brown rats
squeezing from hidey-holes all over the boat. These four-footed
travelers did bide their time and wait for night. Now in a rigid
formation they slither down mooring ropes on fleshy pink feet,
scaly, ringed tails undulating behind them. In a long snaking
column, these creatures slink and sneak across the meadow to the
village following trails of corn spilled from grain sacks.

chapter **six**

There is no sign of gentry or rats when I wake, but after the revelry of the former and nighttime excursion of the latter, I am not surprised. However, the common folk tumble over cottage doorsteps hauling piles of blankets into the sunshine. These they shake vigorously until clouds of dirt and scraps of straw and multitudes of fleas do spiral above their heads. Then the bedding is spread for airing on the green, along with quantities of crumpled weskits, skirts, and hose, until the grass resembles a giant patchwork quilt.

Their children start a game of Ring Around, tumbling into tangled heaps in the dusty lanes when "they all fall down." When Samuel and his collie drive a dozen bleating sheep through the village, the lads and lassies squeal in alarm and dart behind the cottages. There must not be multitudes of sheep roaming the streets of London, methinks.

None in the village appear to recall Pappy's warning that people such as these fleeing London might spread the plague. But I am much afraid for them. What can I do to still my troubled mind? In desperation I pick up my neglected piece of knitting from the sill and settle cross-legged upon my bed to work on Jack's hose. Holding the wooden needles tight in my sweaty hands, I recite aloud, "in over through off—in over through off—in over through off," but before I have completed even three rows there is a hole in the kingfisher blue yarn and three stitches have disappeared. My fingers ache. My back aches. My legs ache. I toss down the silly stocking and fix myself a beaker of cider.

When I am lured back to the window, Hannah is prodding her cow down Dykes Lane to graze upon the common as she does every day. There is much ado at the Mullin cottage. Amos and Noah heave a wooden table through the front door. Then Noah clatters a chair to the ground and is roundly cuffed by Master Mullin. The boy takes it, his arms hung low, face blank as the rind on a round of cheese.

When Amos hauls a cart from the barn it is obvious their journey will shortly begin, so I must expect that Hannah Mullin will join me soon in the chamber. I most certainly do not look forward to the moment of Hannah's arrival.

Soon Mistress Mullin appears, tugging her cap about her ears and tweaking her apron straight. Her frown is firmly in place as she strides across the green for fresh water and a gossip with

Mistress Goody at the pump. Her voice carries clear through my chamber window.

"Goodly Christian of you to take that family in," she says, nodding to the Londoners sitting in the shade of Mistress Goody's doorstep. They are a motley bunch to be sure, city pale, matted hair, ill fed, and none too clean besides.

"Especially when they have the means to pay," chuckles Mistress Goody, rubbing her hands together. "But I see you are preparing to depart. Rather you than me to tackle such a trek."

"It is worth the effort. To a land of Puritans, we go," boasts Mistress Mullin, "and I leave you well rid of the pale one. With her cottage in a ruin she'll not return." She scowls down Sherborne Lane to the stark stone chimney piece, shimmering in the hot sun.

"Blessing it is, witch that she was," agrees Mistress Goody.

These words send a shudder down my spine. I am not a witch! I am not. These women are ignorant prattleboxes. I slump upon my mattress again desperate to forget their evil words, but in the end I am drawn back to the window.

The skinny little ragamuffin is back from the common, slinking past Mistress Goody's cottage. He stands on tippy-toe running his hand along the window ledge scrounging for pies. He has an uncommon flush on him today that near matches his carroty-top hair.

"Stop, beggar," shouts Mistress Goody, spying the child. She shakes her beefy fist in the air and gathers up her skirts to make chase.

But Mistress Mullin is faster. "Up to no good," she shrieks, tripping over the blankets and capes spread about the grass, in her pursuit of the urchin. She grabs him by the arm and shakes him like a cat with a rat. "Be off with you." She drops her prey, but he lies still. Not moving. Silent as stone, like the birds upon my cottage roof just before they died.

Mistress Goody puffs across the green to examine the bundle of skin and bone lying upon the ground. Then she yelps so loud it near drowns out Joe and his clanging down at the smithy. "Lord in heaven, his neck! A swelling!" She backs away from the fallen child. "It is big as a damson plum and hard as the pit."

Mistress Mullin kneels down and pulls up his tattered shirt. Even I can see clear from my place by the window that he is covered in red blotches. Plague tokens, just as Pappy described. And delivered by the London barge just as he predicted. Now these newcomers are about the village, living in the cottages, breathing the air, sharing food and water. I wring my hands in despair. What will become of these people?

"Who has charge of this child?" shouts Mistress Mullin.

No one answers. The visitors sidle off, clutching their offspring. No one seems to know who the beggar is or how he managed a ride in the barge. So Mistress Mullin and Mistress Goody, too, scurry away from the fallen boy. Their skirts fidget and flick through the dust in their haste to leave him behind.

My heart near breaks in two for the child lying dead in the baking heat outside my window. And I can do naught but pray that God takes the little orphan up to heaven and gives him the love he so sadly lacked here on earth.

I keep watch over his body till around midday I am much relieved to see our vicar Reverend Morton discover the lad. With much gentleness he wraps the puny, pocked body in a piece of sackcloth and carries him from the green to lay him on the bench in the porch beneath my hiding place.

"Master Matty, be quick to dig a grave for this poor unfortunate," he calls. "He should be buried with haste." But Matty's spade makes slow progress in the baked earth beneath the stone wall surrounding the churchyard.

The vicar returns to the green, ringing a handbell. Folks stare morosely at our pastor, clutching the trinkets and potions bought lately from the wandering peddler.

"The youth surely died of plague," says Reverend Morton, "so the illness is brought to our village, and we are indeed in God's hands. Gather now in the church and we will beg God's forgiveness."

"Forgiveness for what, might I ask?" mutters Mistress Mullin, seemingly recovered from her shock. "The Mullin family live a godly life and leave for better parts than this where we will abide under God's true law. No such foolery as crucifixes and bowing in the name of Jesus."

"Mistress Mullin, there is but one God for us all, and we must do what we can to stay this disease now that it is upon us."

The villagers, as well as evacuees both rich and poor, flock obediently beneath my secret chamber into St. Giles much like Old Samuel's sheep. Clods of earth thump and thud upon the ground as Master Matty struggles to spade the hole that will shelter the nameless child.

More than a hundred people are squeezed into the church, hot and sweat drenched, all crammed hard together. Reverend Morton drones on, offering up prayers to God to save us all from the plague. Incense drifts on the heavy hot air, sickly sweet upon my shrunken stomach. Voices rise and fall in prayer, but what can save us now, I wonder, marking yet another day gone by upon the wall.

chapter seven

A few days later I am woken at dawn to the sound of Master Mullin hitching his horse into the traces of the cart, loaded full now with their earthly belongings. I force myself to chew a morsel of stale bread dipped in ale before kneeling at the window to peer over the sill. Amos is astride a roll of bedding, his thick thighs spread like sides of beef. Noah crouches atop a trunk, squinting his beady eyes and scratching his head. Two gormless brothers, knowing not where they go but going where they are bid, unlike Hannah Mullin, who argues her wants and suffers abuse for it. Methinks she will wait for her Jack, no matter how long, no matter the cost.

But where is Hannah? Can it be she is hiding elsewhere on this day of her family's departure? This would please me, for I have no desire to share my tiny chamber with her. She will babble of her plans at every opportunity, and I have no wish to hear more.

"Where's that girl got to, now we are ready to travel forth," hollers Master Mullin. "I'll thrash her clear to kingdom come if she disobey me more."

Mistress Mullin tweaks her cap and pinny, sets her frown in place, and marches through their garden to the cow barn in search of Hannah.

I believe the Mullins will leave no stone unturned to find her, whatever Hannah might believe to the contrary. Likely Amos will be dispatched down the lanes to prod in hedgerows, poke under haystacks, seeking her out. And doltish Noah will clomp behind, aping his brother at every turn. Master Mullin will beat Hannah black and blue when they bring her back. It is always his way.

"Stir yourself, Hannah," shouts Mistress Mullin.

"We leave now," bellows Master Mullin. "Not a moment to lose."

Cottage doors fly open and folks emerge, pulling on doublets and shawls, to see what all the pother is about. The gentry tumble from the tavern and mingle on the green. Even a sleek, fat rat beneath the trough twitches its nose at the goings on. This is a momentous occasion. No one before now has ventured from Letchlade to cross the ocean. I rise up to better observe the fuss and to-do.

"Who has seen our girl?" demands Mistress Mullin. Her frown is furrowed deep as a fresh ploughed field, and her complexion mottles with anger. In her haste to find Hannah, her cap falls askew and a strand of sparse, unwashed hair escapes.

"Perhaps she asks blessing for your journey," suggests Mistress Bramwell, nodding toward St. Giles. A smug smile plays around her mouth, hoping for entertainment, no doubt. Despite the mention of St. Giles, my curiosity is so aroused that I fail to crouch safely below the windowsill again.

Mistress Mullin struts up the path followed by a bevy of spectators. Her wool skirt slaps about her legs, perfectly matching her waspish mood. I press closer to the glass. She glances up. For one spellbinding moment she looks me in the eye. And I cannot help but stare straight back at her.

"Witch! Witch!"

I snatch my toy bird and drop to the floor.

"The pale one is amongst us still!" Mistress Mullin's screams must surely be heard clear down to the river.

"She cannot be," shouts Toby Parker from the tavern.

"We burned her abode," grumbles Amos.

"Broke the spell," splutters Noah.

"A trick of the sun?" But Mistress Bramwell is ruffled. I imagine her pleating the fringe of her shawl with trembling fingers.

"I saw her!" Mistress Mullin cries. "The pale one hovers amongst us. She hexed Noah. Now she steals Hannah."

How can I stay safe? Pressed low beneath the sill clutching my carved bird, I pray for God to help me.

"Witch! Witch!" The throng takes up the chant now. I hear them milling about the churchyard, clambering over gravestones, trampling the brittle grass. "Be gone!" booms a voice. Thank the Lord. It is dear Reverend Morton directly beneath me in the doorway of St. Giles.

"There is a witch in your very church," wails Mistress Mullin. "She has put a spell on my Hannah. Hid the girl from her own flesh and blood."

"There is no witch in this church," fumes Reverend Morton.

"There is I tell you!" shrieks Mistress Mullin. "And we must destroy her before she casts more spells upon us."

"Superstition, Mistress Mullin, foolish superstition. But countenance this. If I do discover Hannah, I will give her sanctuary. I dislike the beatings and belittling she has endured for so long, for so little sin."

"How dare you," sputters Mistress Mullin. "Hannah will pay sore for her behavior."

From my position on the floor I can see the early morning sky streaked with bands of red and orange clouds. Below, I can hear folk gathering but I dare not peep. Then there is a howl of horror as a large white bird beats across the crimson-splotched heavens directly outside my window. In the peculiar light its wings take on a rosy tinge. My fingers slacken and my toy plinks on the stone floor—my toy bird that so resembles this bird whirling past my window.

"Do you see?" gurgles a thick and phlegmy voice that I recognize to be Joe. "'Tis the same bird as came when the pale one were born."

"That bird is the Devil himself!" howls Mistress Mullin.

The bird screeches.

I struggle to my knees clutching the windowsill just in time to see Mistress Mullin stagger a short way down the path with her arms stretched out, palms up, and fingers taut. She falters and spins on her toes to face the Church of St. Giles once more. An expression of pure astonishment crosses her face, wiping away her perpetual frown. Then she topples upon the ground, and I know that she is dead. Dead of the plague.

All do surround Mistress Mullin, weeping and wailing, cursing and swearing. The foulest threats to be rid of me linger in the humid air. For a moment I am paralyzed by this terrible scene, and then I duck down again. No one would show me mercy, of that I am certain, for they saw Mistress Mullin fall dead minutes after she announced my presence amongst them still—minutes after the mysterious bird appeared.

I imagine Noah to be slumped beside his ma's corpse, confusion clouding his dull face. Except for my mortal fear, I could feel sympathy for his plight. Then I hear Master Mullin bullying and browbeating Reverend Morton in the porch below.

"It is a crime to cast spells!" howls Master Mullin. "And the culprit is in this very church! She brought plague to my wife! The pale one is a witch! I demand justice!" roars Master Mullin.

"Then you need seek it elsewhere," fumes the Reverend Morton, "for I do not dispense the distorted justice that you desire."

I listen to Master Mullin stomping from the porch, still ranting in fury and demanding revenge. It seems he cares little for the welfare of his daughter or even the burial of his wife. And shortly thereafter I am relieved beyond measure to hear the Mullin cart roll out of the village.

The day wears wearily on into evening with no sign of Hannah. The crimson sky makes way for twinkling silver stars. I scratch another mark upon my wall, twenty-seven days now, although my overflowing pisspot is all the proof I need of the time I have endured in this place. I close my eyes and wish for dear Pappy to put his arms around me and assure me that all this is naught but a night terror from which I will wake.

Tap, tap, tap. Tap, tap, tap.

I leap from my mattress. It must be Hannah come to the door. But if I give her shelter now, am I not exposing myself to the plague? May not Hannah already have caught the infection from her ma?

Tap, tap, tapitty tap.

It is not the door. The clamor comes at my window. I pad across the floor in bare feet.

Tap, tapitty, tap, tap, tap.

What I see before me in the moonlight causes me to marvel at the wonder of the Lord. The snow white bird, which caused such consternation this morning, hovers outside my window. Its wings beat rhythmically as it pecks upon the glass panes with a curved, white beak.

"Greetings, magnificent creature of God," I whisper, pushing wide the casement. The bird sweeps through the window, swooshing and swishing like a thrasher in the fields. She floats to a graceful landing at my feet. Never in my life have I seen such a purely white bird. We do match one another well.

I squat beside her. "Where do you come from?"

The bird cocks her head to one side.

"Who are you?"

She blinks gleaming black eyes.

"So Mistress Mullin declared you my familiar?" I whisper.

The bird struts close. There is an odor about her of fresh-blown breezes, clear streams, and lofty beech trees.

"Fie on her," I mutter. "No living creature as exquisite as you can be the Devil in disguise."

My fingers reach out. The feathers on her breast are downy soft. And behind her neck they are sleek as silk.

"Have you come to dine, noble creature of the skies?"

I slice a sliver of smoked eel and place it between us on the floor. The bird sashays forward and dips her head to the fish. Sharp talons anchor it in place. Her white beak tears at the morsel in rapid bobbing motions. How I have missed my creatures of God and the joy they do afford me.

The beautiful bird flutters onto my shoulder. Her claws are dry and warm upon my skin. She nibbles my neck, plucks at my white curls, and croons into my ear.

"If you are sent to watch over me, then you are not the Devil but a guardian angel come from God. And I can think of nothing better," I murmur, "for I am sore alone."

After a few moments the creature launches into the sky. I lean from my window and watch her circle the spinney of trees behind where our cottage once stood before coming to light upon the stark, black chimney piece.

chapter eight

For a whole month not a day passes without a coffin resting in the churchyard awaiting burial; not a day when poor Matty has not toiled to dig another grave; not a day without sawing at the woodcutter's in Dykes Lane, though it is not logs he stacks now but coffins, large and small, piled against his cottage wall.

The scratches march across the wall, so many 'tis hard for me to count.

My food supply is sadly dwindled. Half a loaf of bread, hard as a rock and sprouting mold, a wedge of cheese, a few strips of venison, and some apples. I have but one flagon of ale left to sup.

My only comfort is the magnificent white bird who *tap, tap, tappitty taps* upon my casement each evening. Without her I fear I might die of loneliness. From the river's edge she brings water mint to sweeten my fetid chamber. From the meadows an abundance of dandelion and watercress, which are freshly fragrant upon my tongue. From the woodland she carries ripe strawberries, red bar- berries, and crimson honeysuckle berries, pleasing treats indeed.

There has been no sign of Hannah since before her ma died. If it were not for her hair ribbon tangled in my pocket I swear I would not give her a second thought though my mind is much upon the fate of Pappy and Jack. Have they met? Are they safely on the boat? Away from this dreadful plague? Pray God, it is so.

I struggle this morning with Jack's hose, knitting and purling alternate rows across my needles, but I fear they will do naught to warm his legs, for they possess almost as many holes as my wall bears scratches. I fling the wretched knitting aside.

Shortly before noon I hear the Reverend Morton calling the villagers together on the green. Sipping a beaker of ale, I watch from my window.

"These are terrible times," says the Reverend Morton. He dips his kerchief in the trough and dabs his forehead. "This past month seventeen in our village have died, as well as eleven visitors from London."

I stifle a moan, though I know this fact full well.

"Many of us have fallen victim to the sickness," continues Reverend Morton. "I urge you to keep clean your homes, burn or bury soiled linens belonging to the afflicted, along with your own excrement. Does seem to me this may slow the contagion."

Mistress Goody puts her hands on her hips and snorts like the porker she keeps in the sty behind her cottage.

"Enter God's church," Reverend Morton continues. "Let us pray he can help us escape the evil pestilence that has overtaken us."

There is a sullen silence.

Our vicar sways and clutches the pump to steady himself. I fear he is most unwell. "I bid you to the church," he beseeches, coughing into the kerchief. "We will pray to God to forgive us our sins and spare us more loss."

"We are decided none will set foot in that church again till you rid the place of the pale one," seethes Joe. "The witch that Mistress Mullin did see. The witch that killed her."

At these words I abandon my place by the casement. But I hear the malicious words still, worming their way into my tiny chamber through the cracked open window.

"Rid us of her and the plague will surely disappear," grumbles Toby Potter, who pours ales at the tavern. "That should be clear enough to anyone with half a mind to see."

"Purge us of the evil one," mutters Mistress Bramwell, folding her arms across her chest. "She lurks in the air. I feel it."

"It is the pale one brought blight upon the village, just as Mistress Mullin predicted," agrees Mistress Goody. "The pale one cast a spell that stifled the life from Mistress Mullin, and you did naught to save her."

I listen to gasps erupt and rumble through the crowd, for it is a bold way to speak to a man of God, no matter what the circumstance. Unable to resist, I sneak back to the window.

"I beg you to follow me," says the Reverend Morton, but his voice is hoarse. When he attempts to scoop a handful of water from the trough he coughs instead upon the ground. In horror I see that the dry grass is flecked red with splatters of blood.

"The church is taken by Satan," claims Joe. "See now how the Reverend is marked. Which of us will follow next?"

"I agree we must avoid St. Giles," says Mistress Goody. "And say our prayers by our own hearths in a godly Puritan way. That will keep us safe."

"No one shall enter that place," commands Joe. "I'll make sure on it." He wrenches a cumbersome pistol from his belt, much like the weapon Pappy used in the Civil War, and waves it in the direction of the church. "If the pale one be in there let her starve to death."

I crouch low beneath my sill seething with hatred for this man, but still I keep watch.

The Reverend Morton tries once more to rally his congregation. "I beg you, come pray in the house of the Lord." But he can only totter a few steps before swooning upon the grass. All do recoil from the stricken priest, clutching each other in horror.

"What did I tell you," says Joe, his hands firmly clamped about the pistol.

"But if we leave him there, will not God strike us dead?" wails Mistress Goody.

In response Toby fetches a barrow into which he heaves the poor limp body of Reverend Morton. When he has wheeled him down the path and into the porch, I hear the vicar dumped upon the stone bench. The poor man lies mortally ill below me, and I am helpless to aid him. For I am bound by my word to Pappy, as well as by the dangerous crowd beneath me, to remain hidden in my chamber.

With no thought for the vicar, my neighbors disperse through the lanes. In a very short time Master Goody and Master Bramwell have piled their belongings into carts—chickens stowed in make-shift pens, milk cows and porkers tethered to the shafts. They depart with their families west toward the Welsh hills. The other survivors will quickly follow, of that I am certain.

The gentry, who did naught to help our poor vicar, sneak through the meadow followed by their servants pushing handcarts laden with baggage. No doubt they intend to abandon the poor folk and board the barge for London as quickly as possible.

Soon not a soul will be left in Letchlade.

Only me in the secret chamber.

The wondrous white bird keeping watch down at the spinney.

Joe in his smithy.

And an abundance of bloated rats, feasting in a listless way about the lanes and hedgerows.

chapter nine

Night after night Joe prowls the boundary wall of St. Giles, the pistol stuck in his belt, despite he has yet to set eyes on me and has no proof that I am here at all, beyond his belief in the ravings of heartless Mistress Mullin.

Tonight I have counted sixty scratches on my wall, and I think I will cease to mark the passage of time, for I fear I shall shortly perish despite the treats my bird does bring me. Only three strips of venison are left on my shelf, a small chunk of cheese, and half a flagon of ale. The sun sets low in the sky so I know that autumn is now upon us despite the persistent heat.

An owl hoots in the old oak tree behind Hannah's barn. I sip a musty beaker of ale and cast my eyes upon the Mullin cottage, shuttered and deserted. The barn behind is bathed in shadow.

Then my flesh prickles—up and down my spine, along my arms and legs—for boots smack on the hard ground, and I hear a sigh, deep and desolate as a winter wind soughing upon the wolds.

Is it a nonsense? Surely I must imagine the shadowy figure in a wide-brimmed hat and flowing cape, outlined against the rising moon, creeping through the vegetable garden and into the cow barn.

But in truth the figure resembles Jack. How can this be? Is he not safe on the boat with Pappy? If I were not so a-feared of Joe I might ignore Pappy's instructions to stay in my chamber and hurtle across the green to discover for myself if my imagination runs amok, for I yearn so to see dear Jack again.

I settle back upon my mattress, but my mind will not rest as it frets over Pappy and Jack, my dwindling supplies, and those dark shadows outside Hannah's barn. Then I hear a footfall upon my stairwell. Dear God! Is it Joe? No. A bucket is set upon the steps. Only one person would think to do such a thing. Hannah Mullin. She comes at last after all this time.

"What kept you?" I snap, jumping up. There is a slight fragrance of rose petals so I know that it is Hannah, despite the dense silence that lurks on the other side of the oaken door.

"Hannah, answer me. I know 'tis you."

"I fear I have the plague," she whispers.

The plague. I step backward, sore afraid. How dare Hannah Mullin bring the plague to my door? Have I not endured agonies to keep myself isolated from this curse? I do not wish to die now.

I will not. I clench my fists, and my knuckles gleam silver in the moonlight.

"Why did you not come before you were infected?" I snap at her again.

"Your pa ordered you keep to yourself, and I decided it best to wait till he delivered my ribbon to Jack." She pauses, her voice raspy and hoarse. "You did hand on the token, Gwen? Did you not?"

The yellow hair ribbon is a leaden weight in my pocket, just like my heart is a leaden weight in my chest. But I am not about to confess its whereabouts now.

"Yes," I lie. "Of course I did."

"I thought to wait for Jack upon the wolds." Hannah lurches against the door as if to steady herself. "For I could see below me the roads clogged with people. Never such crowds have I seen, all in a panic to escape the plague." She gasps for breath. "I fell in with an old widow woman wandering on the hills. But she was most poorly. I wrapped her in my shawl. . ." Hannah's voice fades into the thick plank door separating us. "Gwendoline, she died in my arms."

"Hannah, your mother too has died of this scourge. Your father and brothers left the village long since. They did not wait on you."

Does she hear me? Does this news grieve her, despite her family's cruel ways? Her breath is labored, rattling in her chest something fearsome. I fancy the door itself does shimmy.

"Do you suppose Jack has my ribbon now?" she weeps. "Might he still return? For I wish to cast a last look upon his dear face before I go to our Lord."

God's thunder, I am sick of her token. I pluck the wretched
yellow ribbon from my pocket and toss it on my windowsill. How
I wish I had done her bidding and rid myself of it last July.

"I suffer such chills and delirium," Hannah moans. "Help
me, please—"

"Hannah, I cannot tend you," I cry. "My eyes have settled on so
many dead. I do not want to die in such a way. Not after all these
weeks hid in this place."

Besides, I promised Pappy—*no matter what you see, no matter
what you hear, stay*—'tis not fair of Hannah to beg me so.

"Rest in the church, Hannah," I mutter. "All but Joe are
gone now. He will not enter, for he believes I have cast a spell
upon St. Giles."

"I ail badly, Gwendoline."

"I can do naught for you."

"*Please* help me, Gwendoline, *please*." Hannah's fingers brush
upon the door, soft as moths upon the casement. "You can heal
me. I know you can."

A tear trickles down my cheek. My mammy would not have
left Hannah Mullin to endure this affliction alone, I am sure.
How can I ignore her suffering? I remember the warmth of
Pappy's hands about my cheeks—*you are a special child, indeed.
Blessed with a gift of healing.*

Despite how I wished that Jack had chosen me instead of
Hannah, how petty it all seems now that she ails so. Though in
truth I doubt Hannah can be cured of this illness.

I shiver so I can scarce keep to my feet.

❧ Chapter Nine ❦

My fingers reach for the latch on the door that separates me
from Hannah Mullin. If I open it, I risk suffering the same fate as
so many others. But if I do not, I leave Hannah to die.

While I stand all of a dither, Hannah slumps against the door
like a sack of flour.

chapter *ten*

I throw caution to the winds and thrust open my chamber
door. Hannah is fallen in a heap on the top stair. Perspiration
streams in rivulets down her cheeks and her skin is fire hot
with fever.

I scoop her into my arms and fetch her down the twisting
staircase into the church. It is no easy task. My legs are weak from
lack of nourishment and quiver badly. But the cool nave of St.
Giles is welcome after my hot, fetid chamber.

Where best to care for her stricken body? I lay her on a pew
and look about me. I need a safe place. To the left of the altar is
the vestry door, shielded somewhat from view should Joe take
it upon himself to enter the church after all. With both hands I
turn the huge iron key, push open the door, and step down into

the tiny room. On the opposite wall is a deeply recessed window and another smaller door leading into the churchyard. Reverend Morton's ornamental vestments hang on black metal hooks. I take the nearest, embroidered with gold and purple threads, and make Hannah a bed upon the floor.

I fetch her hot smoldering body from the pew and remove her wool skirt and bodice with trembling fingers. Her undergarments are horribly soiled, which causes me to retch violently, but continue I must. When I have removed them down to her naked skin I am sore afraid. In her groin is a most terrible swelling and two more are in her armpits, tight and red and hard to the touch. Hannah groans with pain when my fingers brush against them.

I am as close to this blight now as can be, and it will be God's will if I live or die. I return to my chamber to fetch the water brought by Hannah, a piece of tallow soap, and a fresh shift of my own to put upon her.

In the vestry cupboard is a pile of laundered altar cloths, and I tear one into strips that I might bathe her body clean. She is withered away; her poor arms and legs are thin as twigs and her spine knotted as alder bark. Not much to remind me of the vibrant lassie twirling around the maypole.

In the cupboard I discover a fragrant anointing oil, which I smooth upon her poor sick body. When she smells sweet again, I dress her in my laundered shift and cover her in another cloth.

I recall the Reverend Morton's words of warning to the villagers— *remove soiled linens from the house.* Had he made some connection when he ordered these garments to be destroyed? I roll Hannah's foul clothing tight. If he was right, then I must be rid of this bundle and be quick about it. I slip through the vestry door.

'Tis my first venture to the outside world since late July, but there is no time to savor the fresh air. When I am sure that Joe is patrolling on the west side of the church, I hurl the parcel as far as I can between the headstones. May God forgive me, but it must be gone from us and cannot hurt the dead.

"I am parched bad," Hannah murmurs when I return to her side. Her fingers flit upon the fresh white cloth like fledgling birds.

The blessed cupboard yields five vessels of communion wine and I pour some into a chalice. Hannah must have liquid, and this will fortify her well. God would not wish her to suffer, of that I am certain.

I raise Hannah's head and hold the golden goblet to her lips. "Drink, it will quench your thirst." She sips a drop. Wine dribbles down her chin and leaves a round stain, red as my petticoat frill, upon the altar cloth. "More, to put you in a goodly sleep." Hannah gulps till the cup is empty. The wine does seem to aid her.

"Gwendoline, I am so grateful," she whispers. "Can you heal me of this dreadful sickness?"

Do I tell her more lies? For I am certain sure there is no way I can cause the buboes to disappear. "Hannah, I fear that I cannot."

"Then I will not live to see my Jack again." What a wealth of longing there is in Hannah's deep brown eyes. "Tell Jack I loved him to distraction," she murmurs in a most pitiable way, like a newborn kitten after milk.

When I am certain she sleeps, I step into the church. Shafts of moonlight spill from the high windows and do feel like the consoling fingers of God upon my cheeks. I am desperate to atone for the spite I felt toward Hannah. Before it is too late.

I speed upstairs to my secret chamber and snatch the yellow ribbon from the sill. Is it possible I can still deliver her token after all this time? I peek out of the window. Not a shadow nor a movement do I spy about the Mullin barn. But I must believe that it was Jack I saw. I *must*.

I open the casement and whistle softly. Wings swoosh through the thick humid air, and my white bird flutters into the chamber. She dances on the floor. Her claws scritch and scratch on the flagstones.

"Noble creature of God, seek Jack for me."

She pecks my toes and caws deep in her throat.

I hunker down and dangle Hannah's yellow ribbon before her sharp hooked beak. "Find Jack," I beseech.

She snatches the ribbon from my fingers and flaps her wings.

"Fetch him back," I beg.

My white rook floats through the window, trailing the yellow ribbon in her beak. She flies across the green and hovers above the Mullin cottage. Is Jack there? But my bird glides higher and soars above the wolds where Samuel's sheep still dot the hills. I stand for an age at my window caressing my toy bird, warm and smooth. *Bring him home*, I pray, *bring him home*.

When I descend my secret stairs once more, I am met by the sight and sound of Bedlam. Hannah has risen from her sickbed, torn off the shift, and careens naked up and down the aisle. She screams for God to relieve her pain. In her delirium she tears at her hair and slams into pews, bruising her already battered body. She is consumed by the evil fever for she shouts curses and uses sundry words never uttered by decent folk.

If Joe does hear this ghastly din he will be more than ever convinced the Devil resides in St. Giles. I can do naught to stop Hannah till at last she collapses at the foot of the altar. I manage to wrap her sickly body once again, carry her back into the vestry, and lay her down upon her bed of vestments.

"Hannah, sup more wine. Will calm you down and help you sleep."

I keep watch by Hannah's bedside, all the while soothing her brow with oil, and pray to God my bird will guide Jack back to both of us.

At dawn, assuring myself that Joe is not in sight, I slip outside and hoist my skirt behind the Penance Stone to release a warm stream of piss. Does feel good indeed to be done with my odorous chamber pot at last.

Then from the front of the church I hear the rich rumble of a dear and cherished voice. I creep around the corner of St. Giles, peering through the early morning light, and discover that my prayers are answered! It is Jack indeed, holding his arms high in the air. And with good reason. Joe prods his clumsy weapon into Jack's chest.

"God's thunder, man, let me past," pleads Jack.

"No one steps into that evil place," bellows Joe.

"Out of my way," begs Jack. "Please."

"St. Giles is taken by the Devil," shouts Joe. "He cast spells all night long. Such cussing and swearing—"

My feet scarce touch the ground as I flee to the vestry, for the memory of poor out-of-her-head Hannah last evening, cavorting up and down the nave, has given me a notion. I tear off my skirt and blouse and grab a starched white altar cloth. Thank God Reverend Morton did keep a goodly stock. I wrap it around and around my body much as the Roman invaders dressed so many years past, but I am careful to leave bare my milky neck and arms, as well as remove my cap so that my near-white hair may cascade to my waist. I dart back along the path to the porch door.

"Be gone, Jack Marlow, if you know what's good for you," yells Joe.

Jack hesitates.

"There's not a soul left in this beleaguered village. 'Tis for your own good I do not let you near."

Jack steps back a pace.

"The pale one brought plague among us, and she was seen in this very church. She will give you the plague, I tell you."

Jack must not leave. He must not! Hannah must set eyes upon him once more; it is the only way I can make amends for my envy and malice.

"Indeed I will," I sing, prancing down the churchyard path

in my fantastical garb. "I will give you the plague, the plague, the plague—"

"Gwendoline," Jack cries. "Dear God, what—"

Joe howls at the sight of me.

"Beware of my witchy ways," I chant. "If you wish for a witch, you begat a witch!"

The sun rises clear now. I stand still as a statue upon the path for I know that it beams upon my snow white costume, skin, and hair. Joe will remember well Mistress Mullin's opinion of mist gray eyes and powdery lashes set in a pale round face. Witchy indeed must I appear to Joe.

"Take heed, have a care," I croon. "For this witch do lay you bare."

My beloved white bird watches over me well. She spins out of the heavens and launches at Joe with ungodly screeching.

"And cast a spell that's truly fair!" I finish in triumph.

Joe stumbles down the path, dropping his pistol with an almighty clatter. Before he can think to retrieve it, Jack snatches up the weapon and fixes it into the folds of his cape. "Good riddance!" he shouts.

All the while my rook pursues Joe, squawking and shrieking. She dips low, striking at his neck and arms with her sharp beak. Joe waddles fast as he can on his fat, flat feet, a-feared for his life.

Jack grabs me and hugs me tight. I breathe his musky scent. I can scarce believe his presence.

"What on God's good earth is happening here?" he asks, winding a strand of my loose hair between his fingers. "I swear that curious bird led me here."

"That curious bird is my guardian angel, Jack. She watches over me in the secret chamber where I have been hid." I grasp Jack's arm and shake him hard. "But where, oh where, have you been? Pappy went downriver in search of you."

"Later, Gwen, all later. There is so much I do not understand. I fear the Mullins have gone." He pulls Hannah's ribbon from his pocket. "Did Hannah leave any word? Any word at all?"

I draw him close. "Jack, you must be brave for the worst thing that can happen in all the world is happening inside St. Giles."

Jack mashes his fists against his ears, but I wrench them free. "You *must* hear me, Jack, for I can bear it alone no more. Hannah is with me in St. Giles."

Hope gleams in his eyes, green and dense as woodland moss.

"But Jack, she suffers the plague, and I fear she is close to the end."

Clutching my witchy garb about me, I drag him through the vestry door. Jack gazes upon his poor sick girl in disbelief. She is horribly thin, but her hair is smoothed about her shoulders and blessedly the swellings are hid beneath her shift, for they are hideous to look upon.

"Is there any hope?" He slumps to his knees beside Hannah.

I shake my head. "She is mortal ill."

Jack lies upon the vestment to gaze into the ravished face of his love. He strokes her raven hair and nuzzles into her withered neck.

Hannah's eyes open. "Jack, my love, my own. . . You came. . . I believed you would. . ." Her voice is thin as mist upon a dawn river.

Jack raises her up in his arms and sobs into her wasted shoulder.

"Remember me with joy," Hannah gulps, "for I have not long now."

chapter eleven

There is such a love between Hannah and Jack that I can bear it no more and leave them alone to share their last few hours together.

My chamber stays stifling hot. But at least I can be rid of my piss pot at last. Slipping into bodice and skirt I carry the offensive contents into the churchyard and cast them into the darkest, farthest corner.

Back in my room I spy my last apple and I pick up my knife, intending to slice the remaining sweetmeat. But when I pluck it from the shelf I discover the fruit gone rotten.

Spoiled. Like all else around me: Hannah Mullin is close to death, Jack and I are likely to die of plague, too, and God knows what has become of dear Pappy. In a rage of frustration and grief I raise my knife high in the air and stab the decayed fruit. Splat! My clean bodice is sprayed with a soft brown slop from the foul apple.

I stare at the sopping mess. I stare at the knife in my hand. I flick it back and forth. I finger the sharp blade. Such thoughts scuttle and scurry about my head that I am breathless. If Pappy is right—*you are a special child, blessed with a gift of healing*— can I save Hannah after all? With the aid of this knife, I think I might indeed.

Time is short. I fling off my stained bodice and pull on clean clothing. Between the bands of my skirt and pinny I thrust the knife.

Night draws nigh and I must have light to carry out my plan. As if God hears my need, there is Joe staggering down Sherborne Lane clutching a flaming torch. The silly fool intends to burn down St. Giles, just like he destroyed my home.

I flee down my secret stairs, pass through the porch containing the putrid, fly-covered body of poor Reverend Morton, and hasten onto the path.

What I perceive at once is that Joe suffers the plague. His head is distorted by a swelling on his neck. His eyes are wild and bulge with hatred.

"I'll be done with you once and for all, evil one," he rasps.

"Go ahead, Joe, throw your torch," I jeer. "Aim it well!"

"May you roast in hell for your sins," he snarls, swaying with fever.

The flaming branch crackles and snaps in the hot night.

"Methinks you cannot harm a witch, Joe. No matter how hard you try."

"If it's the last thing I do, I will take your life," he gasps, "just like your wretched ma and her witchy potions took the life of my family." He reels back and forth like a drunkard. "You are sent by Satan."

"You can hurt me no more," I bait him further. "It is a terrible thing you did to burn down my pappy's home." I tread slowly toward him. I raise my right arm and point direct at his heart. "But now I cast a spell on you that is the very, very last."

Goaded beyond reason he steadies himself against a gravestone. Hatred is etched into his bleak brow. Spite gleams in his fevered face. Finally he hoists the torch above his head and heaves. Thanks be to God, the effort finishes him for good. He pitches backward, his eyes roll back in his head, and he falls dead upon the path.

The blazing torch careens over my head and comes to rest against the porch. Sparks ignite the dry shriveled grass beneath the walls, and I stamp hard with my clogs to put out the snaking trails of fire. When I am sure that none remain, I grab the burning torch and tumble into St. Giles.

Black shadows streak the stone walls. Jack hovers over poor sick Hannah bathing her forehead, though she moans and mewls in pain.

"Jack," I shout. "Joe has just died of the plague."

"Leave us be, Gwendoline," says a weary Jack.

"I cannot for I know what I must do."

I fumble in the cupboard and, praise the Lord, I remembered correctly. There lay six large altar candles. Most necessary to assist me in my purpose.

"Arrange these candles about Hannah's bed," I order. My voice echoes around the tiny room.

"Gwen, for pity's sake, cannot you leave—"

"Nay! It is now or never. Do as I bid."

Jack heaves to his feet and takes the holy candles one at a time from the cupboard. I light each from the flaming torch in my fist, then remove it to the baptismal font in the church where it can burn itself out without causing harm.

I hold fast to Jack. "I am going to try to save Hannah," I say. "I am going to cut open her swellings." I pluck the knife from my waistband. "Perhaps I can release the poison trapped within."

The blade gleams in the candlelight. Jack recoils in horror. Blood drains from his cheeks. "Never. I cannot let you hurt her."

"Will not be more than the pain she endures now, Jack. It is the only hope to keep Hannah alive." Her eyes are closed, and she is far, far away from us. Time runs out like shadow on a sundial.

"Your pappy calls you an angel here on earth girl." Jack studies me, his face tired and drained. "Do you truly have the gift of healing? Can you truly save her? Can you do this for Hannah?"

"For all of us, Jack. I have not always been an angel here on earth." And it is true. But if I can do this thing it might absolve me of all the jealousies and resentments, so I can be an angel girl once more. This I truly long for.

"Jack, leave me now to do this thing."

The candles sizzle. Splotchy shapes skitter up the walls. Melted tallow masks well the odor of death that hangs in the room like rotting flowers.

"Go to the river. Search me some sickle-wort plants that I can make a salve for Hannah's sores." I drag his cloak about his shoulders. "Go, Jack."

With a jerk of his head, Jack pulls himself together. He bends to kiss Hannah's forehead and finally does as I bid.

When he disappears into the darkness, I take the tallow soap and scrub my hands in the bucket of water. Then I think to do the same with my knife. Kneeling beside Hannah's tortured body I peel back her shift and gaze upon the swelling in her groin.

I think on the apple. How the decayed part gave beneath the blade and how the brown sap oozed out. I place my hand upon the swelling and press my fingers on it piece by piece. Hannah writhes in agony. It is grossly large and horrible hard like an autumn chestnut, but I persevere, bearing upon each portion with care. Hannah shrieks. I stop and raise her head to make her sup more wine. "Drink," I whisper. "Keep drinking. Will put you to sleep." At last she lays her head back in a stupor.

I return to the lump in her groin and begin my probing yet again. At last.

A softer, more malleable spot. I pick up my knife. My hand shakes like alder trees in a spring blow, but I take the point of the blade and hold it close to the softness in the swollen mass. I shut my eyes, take a deep breath, and slice deep.

Hannah howls.

A foul and stinking bloody liquid pours out upon her bedding. Hannah screams again like a rabbit in the jaws of a fox.

I hold my trembling hand to my nose and mouth. It is badly worse than a nest of abandoned and rotten eggs. Much worse. But I know I must remove all of this ghastly pus if she is to survive, and I press hard with my other hand upon the swelling to release the evil poison. It does spurt out. Hannah faints clear away. And I am goodly glad. For there are two more swellings in her armpits, which must be got to.

Sweat pours from my brow. With courage I did not know I possessed, I pull the soiled and stinking shift from her body and raise her arms. With my knife I do repeat the same, slipping deep into the growths where softest and pressing out the noxious venom upon the bedding.

Hannah still breathes. I wash her shriveled body once more, as well as my own. Then I pray to God as I have never prayed before that I have saved her life.

chapter *twelve*

$\mathcal{E}$xhausted beyond measure, I roll up Hannah's foul linens and toss them far into the night. The sun is rising when Jack returns bearing an armful of sickle-worts. He tosses them into my arms and crouches down beside Hannah. "Leave her be, Jack. She sleeps well. The poison is drained."

"I can scarce believe you did this thing."

I can scarce believe it, either. But somehow it did seem a simple and wise act to rid Hannah of the foul venom. Pray God my instinct was correct. I snap the stem from a single sickle-wort and mash the root in a basin with my knuckles, adding drops of oil till I have a potion to spread upon Hannah's wounds.

"This will ease her pain," I mutter.

Jack dips into the pockets of his cape and pulls out three fresh eggs, for all the world like a magician at the Bibury Fair. "Stray chickens still scrabble in the abandoned gardens and lay well along the hedgerows."

"Thank God," I say, "else we would die of starvation, never mind the plague." I crack an egg into a silver chalice and offer it to Jack. "Sup, dear Jack. For you must survive for Hannah's sake as well as mine."

I do the same, and the egg tastes like manna from heaven.

"It is time to tell me all," I say, pulling Jack into a corner of the vestry. "For Pappy waited in vain for you under Osney Bridge last summer."

We lean against the cool stone wall. I long to rest my head upon his shoulder as I did when we were youngsters, but I remind myself that it was not I Jack chose to fetch away.

Jack rubs his fist in dusty circles on the floor. "I had left Oxford for Bampton with the master before that time," says Jack. "He had kin in that village and was determined to escape the plague. In truth I did not mind, for it put me nearer to my girl. But you must believe I sent word to the river for your pappy. I did not forget him. It must not have been delivered."

"Was not. Pappy was sore afraid. He insisted on hiding me in the secret chamber. Then he set off for Oxford again, to seek you out and keep you on the boat till the plague was over."

"Oh, Gwen, this is worrying news." Jack shakes his head. "For by my reckoning it is close to October now. What has happened that he has not returned to shelter with you? Pray God he has not succumbed to this dreadful disease. He has always been as true a father as anyone could wish for."

Surely when Pappy could not find Jack, he would have had the good sense to stay upon the river anyway, well removed from those infected. I must believe it. I must.

"What happened, Jack, when you reached Bampton?"

"All was well till recently. Then the Master's family began to sicken, and he released me from contract that I might continue on to Letchlade. I reached home two nights past to discover our cottage burned to the ground. What was I to think but that you and your pappy did perish in some terrible accident?" Jack twists Hannah's yellow ribbon between his fingers. "And it was clear the Mullin family were gone. Their cottage shuttered. The barn abandoned. I fled to the wolds, too stricken with grief to think of looking in our secret chamber for Hannah."

"I have been hid here since late July," I whisper. "I thought I might go mad with loneliness. But thank the Lord my bird did bring you back."

"Aye, it did indeed. It flashed down from the heavens bearing Hannah's yellow ribbon in its beak and did guide me here." All the time Jack speaks, he twists the ribbon into knots and keeps an eye upon his lassie. "Have you truly healed her of this dreadful affliction?"

"I do not know, Jack," I whisper, "for I have watched many in the village die, all in different ways. Yet some lucky few who were exposed bore no ill at all from it."

"Then let us hope we have that same protection," sighs Jack.

"Regardless of our fates, Hannah will need more than an egg to sustain her recovery," I say. "Stay with her. I will venture forth in search of food."

Outside, moisture hangs thick in the air. A border of dark clouds hover above the wolds. Perhaps at last God will bring rain to break this oppressive heat we have suffered so long. Then autumn can properly begin.

How strange, after such a time, to stand upon the green. I feel no fear now as I pump water at the trough and soak my face and arms in the cool clear liquid. Then I gulp and gulp till my belly swells.

My legs are trembly with hunger, but I walk slowly through the abandoned village. The White Hart sits idle. Its great oak door grinds and grates on a squeaky hinge. A barrel of ale has long since dripped its contents into the dry earth. Several rats lie dead upon the doorstep.

I shield my eyes to gaze down Sherborne Lane. In the spinney behind the ruin of my cottage, the elms are dotted with vacant nests where the rooks once roosted. They are not unlike the vacant cottages where the villagers once dwelt. Neither birds nor folk took heed of the pending disaster till their fates were sealed.

When I pass Hannah's cottage I fancy I can still hear the snap of Mistress Mullin's spindle sticks. I tread down the weed-choked lanes, through the woods, and onto my beloved wolds. Little did I believe to ever again feel a fresh breeze upon my cheek, or hear birdsong in the air, or smell fragrant red clover. So intent am I on such joys that I tumble headlong into dear Old Samuel, who is guiding a ewe into a fold.

"Gwendoline Riston, you are alive!" He grasps my shoulders. "I did wonder if any had survived down there in the village."

"And you survived, too." I kiss his gaunt cheeks. "I am well pleased."

He chuckles deep in his throat. "When Joe ordered everyone to kill their dogs I took to the hills. What nonsense that man talks."

"No more, Samuel. He's dead of the plague."

Samuel scratches his stubbly chin. His collie noses for a treat and I offer my empty palms to show there is naught for him.

"You look famished half to death, child," says Samuel, guiding me into the fold beside the curly, bleating sheep. "Sit ye down."

He grabs the ewe and squirts fresh milk from her teats into a beaker. Never did a drink taste sweeter, slipping and sliding down my throat.

"Where have you been all this time, lass?"

"Hid well, Samuel. Hid well."

"And your pa, child, what of him?"

I fear the leaden weight that is my heart will plummet upon the grass. "I know nothing of Pappy's whereabouts." When I speak these words I understand that Jack was right to ponder his well-being. But I am loath to accept that Pappy is lost to the plague.

"Oh, child, I still fear for ye," Samuel sighs. "With autumn gales about to blow, those who fled will return from the hills. And they'll seek someone to blame other than God for this disaster. Without your pa to defend you—"

"Jack did return," I whisper.

"And he will protect you, eh?"

"Samuel," I cry, "surely you do not think Jack would leave me. Not with Pappy missing."

"Makes no odds. Jack Marlow will set his own needs above yours. You mark my words. He's a selfish one in my opinion." Samuel gazes at me out of sad rheumy eyes. "Listen to me, lassie. Seek refuge elsewhere, and quickly. Before the weather turns."

"No matter your opinion, I cannot. For I have Hannah Mullin with me, mortal sick."

"Will she survive it?" Samuel nudges the ewe aside and hunches down beside me. "You think it likely?"

"I believe she has a chance." I clench the beaker tight. "I did drain her swellings and remove the poison from her."

"You've the gift child—a natural healer just like your ma." Samuel nods his grizzled head. "I've always known it. Since you were knee-high to a grasshopper, communing with your creatures of God by Robert Riston's cottage door."

"I *will* nurse her back to health," I whisper, wiping my fingers around the rim of the beaker. "I must." The collie licks the cream from my fingers, his tongue a loving comfort on my skin.

"Then you'll be needing these, lassie," grunts Samuel, holding out a basket of brambles, fresh picked. "Go tend Hannah Mullin."

chapter *thirteen*

I am tired to death of St. Giles, but I fear it is much too soon to move Hannah. And despite my brave words, I do not yet know if what I did was enough to save her life.

"Gwendoline, come quick," shouts Jack from the vestry. "Hannah's fever has cooled. She took an egg. Supped it down a treat."

Hannah's brow is cool indeed. She opens her deep brown eyes and looks not at me, but into the face of her beloved. Her smile is enough to light the world, I do declare. Can she truly be well? Is it possible I have healed her of the plague? Dear God, let it be true. But all the same her eyes shine bright. Too bright, perhaps?

"I love you, Hannah," Jack whispers in her ear. "More than life itself."

"And I you."

Hannah Mullin is frail beneath her wraps. Jack dips toward her bed of priestly robes to kiss her cheek. "You are saved, dear Hannah," he murmurs.

But I am not certain yet. For I have observed the disease take odd twists and turns, and each person die in a different way. I think on Hannah's mother, perfectly fine that morning, struck dead by noon. She had not the swellings that I could tell, but tokens were upon her skin. Reverend Morton I know not other than the coughing of blood. The ragamuffin would seem did have it all. Joe suffered a brief rash. What of the other villagers who died? Some I know were ill for days, others but a short while. Most of all, it is a mystery indeed why some seem resistant to all the vagaries of the plague.

I nudge Jack aside and kneel beside the makeshift bed. "Hannah, I bring you a treat. Fresh berries from the hedgerows."

But she is silent now. Weak as a newborn.

Thunder rumbles upon the wolds. Rain will not be long in coming.

"Urge her to eat," I whisper to Jack. "She must eat or surely die."

Jack presses a plump berry between Hannah's lips and purple juice dribbles on her chin. "Remember when we gathered brambles?" he murmurs. "When we gobbled overmuch and suffered bellyaches?" Her lips part a mite, and she licks the juice with a cracked and sickly tongue.

"Good lass." Jack kisses her brow. "It was Gwendoline who saved you. I could not watch her drain your swellings, but that is what she did."

Hannah's eyes open wide. "Gwendoline, you have proved a dear friend. You did send my token. You risked all to tend me with your healing ways." Her voice is thin as a river reed.

"Did seem the only thing to do," I mutter, hoping my voice does not betray the lie. It took me long enough to be a friend, but what need is there for Hannah to know this now?

Lightning flashes across the sky.

"You must both survive this curse," she breathes.

"Like you, Hannah," murmurs Jack, "Like you did survive."

But Hannah chews upon her lower lip. "Jack, if I do not, for I may not, you must not grieve forever."

Tears leak from his eyes and he cannot still them.

"Love again. It is the most wondrous gift you can bestow." Hannah's eyelids droop. She has not the strength to keep them open. "Promise me."

"My dearest girl. Let us talk of our future," begs Jack.

Thunder claps closer.

"We will yet wed," Jack whispers into her ear. "And have our babes. Did I not promise as much when I fetched you away last May Day? The most beautiful girl ever kissed by morning dew."

Hannah sighs from the depth of her soul. "But if we cannot wed, take the Mullin cottage for you have no other." Tiny tear beads squeeze beneath her dark lashes. "It is yours. Please, please." Hannah gasps for air. "Promise me."

"All right, my dearest girl. Do not fret. We will inhabit the cottage together."

"And Gwendoline, too," she gulps.

"Gwendoline, too," Jack mumbles.

Hannah does not forget me. Despite she guessed my desire to be fetched away by Jack. But none of it matters now. I mix another concoction of sickle-wort root and oil. I rub the salve into Hannah's sores and sing softly.

> *Who will come and fetch her away?*
> *Fetch her away, fetch her away,*
> *Who will come and fetch her away?*
> *On a dew-kissed May Day morning.*

"Thank you, Gwendoline, fairest friend," Hannah murmurs. "Such a calming do I feel now."

Thunder hurtles across the heavens and lightning illuminates the room.

Raindrops drum upon the windowpane. Hannah reaches for my hand across her bed of priestly vestments. "Rain at last," she murmurs.

> *Handsome Jack will fetch her away,*
> *Fetch her away, fetch her away,*
> *Handsome Jack will fetch her away,*
> *On a dew-kissed May Day morning.*

I slip through the vestry door into the churchyard. I raise my face to heaven, tug off my cap, and run my fingers through my hair. A torrent beats upon my forehead, nose, and cheeks. I open wide my mouth and gulp the glorious water pouring out of the sky. Fresh blessed by God.

"Jack, raise me up," I hear Hannah beg. "I so want God's cleansing rain upon my flesh." Her voice is light as a dandelion puff blowing across the meadow.

"Do not move her, Jack," I call. "She is not rested enough."

"It can do no harm to bring my girl to the door," Jack pleads.

My mind is a turmoil. It is much too soon to move her. "Leave her be upon the bed," I warn. Thunder explodes across the wolds. Lightning cracks.

I think to prop open the vestry door so that Hannah might feel sprays of rain wash across her wasted body.

"Only for a moment," Jack calls.

"Nay, let her stay, *please*, Jack—"

But he raises her up in his arms.

"Jack, I pray you, it is too soon—"

Only four strides does he take across the cold stone floor to the open door and one stride into the fresh falling rain before Hannah's head flops from his shoulder like a rag dolly. Her life is gone fast as a gust of wind soughing through the trees.

chapter *fourteen*

I can scarce believe the speed with which the good Lord takes Hannah to him. One moment she gives tongue, begging for the cooling rain upon her skin. The next her life is doused quick as breath upon a candle flame. I have failed to keep Hannah Mullin alive.

Jack holds her in his arms, his face etched with grief. He dips across the threshold once again, leans against the vestry wall, and slides slowly to the ground, all the while cradling Hannah. He croons into her ear, gazes at her shrunken body. Tears stream from his eyes, sopping his doublet and britches, as rain lashes the parched earth.

"Jack, lay Hannah down so I can wash her," I beg, though I still quiver with shock. But I might as well be away atop the wolds for all the notice he takes of me. He is lost in a world of grief.

The storm blows itself out at last, and I collect water in a bucket from the trough. When Jack's bruised eyelids droop and his arms slacken, I gently ease Hannah from his grasp and lay her for the last time upon the bed of robes. I wash Hannah's poor, wasted body and rub anointing oil upon her limbs. Before I wrap Hannah in a crisp white altar cloth, I think to wriggle from my petticoat, edged with the scarlet frill Mistress Mullin so despised, and slip it onto Hannah. A little bit of color and frippery to guide her on her way.

Jack sleeps on, so I return to my secret chamber for the last time. Into my leather satchel I place all my belongings, as well as the precious wooden bird that Pappy carved for me. I conceal my chamber well and return to the vestry. Through the night the candles have all burned to stumps upon the floor, but we shall need them no more.

"Wake. It is time," I whisper, shaking Jack's shoulder gently as the sun rises in the east. A brisk wind blows away remnants of the fearsome hot weather we have endured for so long.

Jack's dull green eyes stare, through me, past me, to some-where so painful I can scarce imagine. Jack is far away, like Hannah on the night I strove to keep her here on earth.

"Hannah waits."

Jack glances upon the shrouded body.

"The storm is done. Let us take her away from the village to where the breezes blow. Where the air is pure. Where she can commune with God."

Without a word he pushes up from the floor, shoves his hat upon his head, dons his cape, and gathers Hannah back into his arms. He bows beneath the vestry door and strides down the path. Hurriedly I add my knife as well as Hannah's comb to the leather satchel. I grab the shovel, which Matty did use to bury the dead, for we shall surely need it to complete our task.

Jack glances not to right or left but stares ahead in a trance, clutching his precious burden. Along Dykes Lane we plod, then the drovers' track across the common. Crops rot in the surrounding fields. Leaves streaked through with gold and red and orange crinkle and curl on the trees in the woods. Holly berries mass in the hedgerows. I shiver, for the berries foretell an early and frigid winter ahead.

Already the air is much cooled. We are scarce out of breath when we reach the wolds. I look down upon our forsaken village wrapped in its gently rolling hills. The river winds through damp lush meadows. The spire of St. Giles soars into the tumultuous sky, blotched with banks of purple cloud. I fancy I do even spy the window of my secret chamber, and the bleak, stark chimney of our cottage, and the spinney with its empty nests.

Jack has spoken not one word since the moment Hannah left us, as if he seeks to join his beloved in her quest for God in his heaven. But he does place dear Hannah upon the ground, sheds his hat and cloak, and grasps the shovel from me with a slight nod.

Hannah's yellow ribbon protrudes from the pocket of his cape and I gather it up and smooth its silky surface between my fingers as I attend her body upon the rain-drenched grass.

Jack digs deep into the earth. The shovel strikes the soft, wet ground—*slap, swat, smack*—over and over till my head does ring with the whack and wallop of it. His doublet is soon drenched in sweat.

When the grave is dug, Jack plucks Hannah from my side and clambers with his burden into the hole to lay his beloved on the wet earth. Earthworms wriggle and slugs slither in the walls around her. I shiver and shiver once more when Jack slumps beside Hannah in her damp dark tomb. He does not leave her. I fear he desires to stay with her forever. I keep watch from the rim of the pit all day long till the sun starts to sink in the sky. I don't know what I must do to coax Jack from this place.

"Jack," I beg him. "Please rise."

His face is hidden in Hannah's shroud, but I know he breathes for I see movement beneath his doublet. And I know he must hear me.

"Let us get to the Mullin cottage before dark. We promised Hannah. At least we will be together. We have each other and we must find food." I am terrified he will ignore me into nightfall.

I am well relieved when Jack finally climbs from the grave. But he pushes past me as if I were a phantom, not there with him on the wolds at all. He wipes soil from his doublet and shrugs into his cape. How can I reach Jack?

"Pappy told me to seek out Lord Bathurst when the plague had run its course. He will provide you a living, I am sure, for he thinks well on Pappy. Did you know the treasure in the secret chamber belonged to his Lordship? And it was Pappy who hid the treasure? The treasure that we played with all those years ago? Did you know—?"

"Stop your prattle, girl!" shouts Jack. "I cannot stand it."

His words sting. They are cruel and cold and frighten me. Why does Jack speak to me in this way?

"You drive me to distraction, Gwendoline."

"We must leave before darkness comes." My voice is urgent with fear.

"No! I cannot stay in Hannah's cottage."

"But you *said* we'd go there."

Jack rakes his hands through his mop of auburn hair. "I said *all* of us, Gwen, not *two* of us."

I clench my fists, and my fingernails dig into the palms of my hands.

"Then we must seek Lord Bathurst."

"I will not go on some ridiculous trek to find his Lordship!"

"Then where, Jack," I plead. "Where will we go? What can we do?" I grab his arms and shake him hard.

"What will *I* do?" shouts Jack, thrusting me away. "Where will *I* go?"

"What about me?" I sob. "What if Pappy is gone forever? Would you leave me with naught in the world? All alone—"

"Not alone, witchy girl." Jack flings his arms in the air. "God's thunder, you have that!"

High above us hovers my faithful white bird. As if bidden, she swoops through the gloom, alights upon my shoulder for a moment, before swirling once more into the sky.

"You cannot call me witchy, you cannot!" I weep. "You have known me since I was a tiny child. You *know* I am not a witch. You *know*!"

"Then why do you commune with animals? Why do you fathom plants in the field?" Jack wails. "Why are you naught but a curse to people! Hannah is dead!"

His words make me reel. "I begged you not to move her, Jack! It was not I who dragged her from her sickbed to her death." My body quivers with anger. I swear he is demented. "How dare you suggest I killed Hannah?"

"*You* wanted to be Queen of the May," he howls in my face. "*You* could not bear to watch Hannah Mullin fetched and feted and crowned by me."

I sink upon the ground, exhausted. It is true. All of it. I *did* want to be Queen of the May. I *was* jealous of Hannah with her perfumed hair, fetched away by Jack and garlanded in May blossom.

"But I wanted to save her, Jack, truly I did. For you. You cannot know how I did dread taking my knife to drain her swellings."

"You helped her on her way—"

"Listen to me!" I shout. "She would surely have died if I had not tried."

And I *know* this is true. "You are consumed with guilt that you might have caused Hannah's death."

Jack lingers on the edge of the grave. His shoulders jerk. His hands shake. He pulls his cape tight as Hannah's shroud. How I wish to enfold him in my arms. Comfort him. Despite his cruel words, I still wish I could make all well in Jack's mind, but I fear I cannot.

"You care well enough for me, do you not, Jack Marlow?" I ask. "How can you abandon me now? Pappy did not abandon you in your time of need."

Jack shoves his trembling hands deep into the pockets of his cape.

"Where will you go?" I yell. "Surely you are not such a coward to discard me like so much chaff?"

"Leave me be," Jack howls. Beneath the thick fabric of his cape his hands stiffen and close tightly. Too late I recall Joe's pistol. He jerks the weapon from its hidden place. "Just leave me be!"

He aims the firearm straight and true at my heart.

Fury bubbles in my gut. "Coward, Jack Marlow," I roar. "Coward indeed that you threaten me. I did not kill Hannah. I tried with all my might to save her."

"Just let me go." His voice is suddenly flat. Once more Jack lowers himself into Hannah's grave.

"Jack, no more foolery," I beg. "Night falls, and we must seek shelter." All the time I try to keep my voice calm. "Pappy would want us to stay together. I know he would. Let's return to the cottage, as Hannah wished. She begged you not to dwell upon the past—"

But all at once the air is split by a single blast.

"No!" I scream. "No, Jack, no!"

Ashy vapors of gunpowder curl up from the damp pit. A stench of death hangs upon the wolds. I fall to the ground beside the gaping pit. Numb. Not a tear more can I shed. Scarce able to believe that Jack did turn the pistol upon himself.

An eternity passes before I am able to gather strength and pick up the shovel. Somehow I manage to heap soil upon Hannah and Jack till they are no more. Nothing but a hummock of newly turned sod upon the windswept wold.

I pluck Hannah's comb from my satchel and weave the yellow ribbon in and out of the tines. When I thrust it into the fresh-turned earth a faint scent of rose petals wafts upon the cold breeze.

chapter *fifteen*

Completely alone in the world, with a cold misery settled in my soul, I journey back to the deserted village guided by a thousand silver stars.

Hannah's cow barn looms before me. And indeed I can travel no farther. Weary beyond belief I nudge open the door and collapse upon a mound of sweet hay.

I must sleep the sleep of the dead. For despite a vague awareness of dawns and dusks, it is many days before I am fully awakened by sunlight blinking through cracks in the barn roof and a fearsome ache in my belly. I am truly famished.

Before I can stir sense into my addled brain, a flash of rust fur darts across the floor. A bushy tail. Two ochre eyes glint in the dusty sunbeams.

"Reynard," I whisper.

The dog fox quivers just as he did a year past when I washed his
torn paw and chewed blue-black whortleberries into a mush to
spit into the wound. Now, clasped between his thin black lips is
a fresh speckled egg. I cup my hands beneath his muzzle and the
gift plops gently into my palms.

This creature of God does not forget me. What a blessing, for
I cannot recall when last I supped. I crack the shell gently with
my thumbnail and drink down the egg. Reynard rests on his
haunches until I am done, then steals from the barn without a
backward glance.

Now I must stir myself if I am to survive. I shake hay from my
hair and skirt and remove the shawl from my satchel before hiding
the bag beneath the mound of hay. I venture outside into the neglected garden, wrapping my shawl tight against the frigid morning
air. The holly berries predicted well a fearsome cold winter ahead.

Before me is the Mullin cottage. A thin frost crusts the latch.
I push down hard and step over the threshold, blinking my eyes
in the murky light. Master Mullin removed his belongings for the
journey to the New World, but something glitters amongst the
ashes in the sooty hearth. The thick metal disc of a spindle-whorl
winks my way. Mistress Mullin does not let go of me yet. The click
and clack of her spindle sticks crackle in my head. The woman
does yet berate me from her grave.

Although the cottage would provide a roof over my head, I cannot linger in this place. Every crevice, every corner, pulses with
injustice. An odor of stale sweat hangs about the empty room, and

malicious motes float on the stagnant air. Spiteful footprints swirl in the dust, thick upon the flagstone floor. Too late I sense danger.

Boots scrape across the attic floor. A cough echoes through the rafters. Malignant words tumble down the steps. Voices I would recognize anywhere.

I am too frightened to move.

"Wake yourself, dunderhead. Make haste to dress," growls Amos Mullin. "We will find her this very day. I feel it in my bones."

"The pale one?" jabbers Noah.

"Yes, you fool, the pale one. Pay attention. The minister Pa employed will prove all grievance against her."

"What of sister?" sputters Noah. "Sister Hannah."

"Hush up. First the pale one must burn in hell for killing our ma."

How many times have I overheard Amos rant thus, as he sought Hannah for some imagined crime. But now she is of no account at all. It is me they are after.

I see black boots set upon the top rung of the ladder and I finally manage to stir my bones. I slip through the cottage door and flee into the neglected gardens of Sherborne Lane. I shuttle beneath hedgerows and crawl between rows of decayed cabbage, hardly knowing what I do except I must avoid the clutches of Hannah's brothers.

I am much confused for I had supposed that Master Mullin took these two dunderheads off across the sea. Did I not hear their cart rumble out of Letchlade with my own ears? And who is this minister that Amos did say will see me doomed?

I reach the abandoned smithy and crouch beneath the wall, for more voices murmur close by—foolish me did think the village deserted. I smell the same unwashed flesh that lingered in the cottage. Two men pace upon the land where my cottage once stood. Dear God in heaven. One is Master Mullin, his stolid square frame and cropped head so familiar to me. The other man I know not, but he wears a shiny, black suit and pointed hat and grips a bible in his right hand, so I suppose him to be the minister that Amos declared would assign me to hell.

"This was her abode?" the minister asks. "You are sure this is where the pale one lived?" His teeth rattle in his head like acorns in a squall.

"Aye." Master Mullin spits. A glob of yellow mucous clings to the base of the blackened chimney piece. "The day she were born a single white bird did alight on this chimney."

"A sure sign of witchery," declares the stranger. "We will have no difficulty proving this case."

"Then let justice be done," barks Master Mullin, "before winter sets in."

"And we are certain she is still in these parts?"

"You saw for yourself where she did cast her spells," Master Mullin grunts. "A circle of fresh-burned candles on the vestry floor is proof enough she did not leave."

I clutch my shawl about my shoulders. What a fool to leave the vestry in disarray. I was so resolved to conceal the chamber I failed to remove evidence elsewhere.

"The survivors of this village cannot winter in the hills without shelter." Master Mullin's breath furls like pipe smoke in the raw air. "But they need proof the pale one's dead afore they return."

"Then we best catch her quick, so she can pay for her sins and life can return to Letchlade."

Their boots crunch through weedy ruts on Sherborne Lane. Master Mullin rummages through an abandoned cottage, searching for me—the pale one. I keep well hid in the tangled gardens.

"Will be easy enough to prove her a witch," boasts the minister. "It is a proven fact witches float on water."

Master Mullin halts. He grabs the man's black cloak in his fists, spittle gathered in the corners of his mouth. "Mistress Mullin saw her once, in the river swimming like a fish—not human at all. And a mass of white hair streaming out behind her in a most unnatural way."

Dear God, I must escape the village and these madmen. For I cannot return to the secret chamber without food and drink to nourish me. I scurry back to the protection of an overgrown garden thinking to hide until I can retrieve my satchel from the barn after dark.

Withered pink rose petals streaked with fine brown veins are scattered about my feet. They so remind me of a vibrant healthy Hannah rinsing her black hair in rose water that I am filled with sadness. I sweep up a handful of petals and stow them in my pocket.

But I hear Amos and Noah enter the garden behind me. Amos thrashes with a scythe, slashing beanstalks and mulberry bushes and thickets of weeds. I must keep moving. I slink through hedges and take refuge in an abandoned chicken coop. The floor is littered with dried manure and downy feathers. The smell is pungent. I hold my shawl to my nostrils, but still my eyes sting.

Through the wooden slats I watch Amos flailing his way forward.

Dim-witted Noah stumps along behind, prodding a pitchfork into haystacks and compost heaps. Suddenly he spies the coop. I squeeze into the darkest dusty corner. As Noah stabs his pitchfork through the slats I slither backward and forward from one end to the other, but my hands and knees disturb piles of molted feathers, and without any warning I sneeze loud as a thunderclap.

"Hey!" Noah drops the fork. He thrusts his arm into the coop and grabs my leg. "Hey!" He pulls hard. "Hey! Hey!"

I hear Amos hurl down his scythe at Noah's shouts.

"Stop," I beg.

He keeps tugging.

"Let me go!" I shriek. "It's Gwendoline Riston!"

In confusion, Noah loosens his grip on my leg. I crawl out of the coop and attempt to scramble away, but as soon as Noah sees me he blinks his weak piggy eyes. "The witch," he splutters, grabbing me by the ankle yet again.

"Nay, Noah, not a witch. 'Tis Gwendoline."

His mouth gapes. "Witch," he babbles.

"Noah, have you forgot me? Robert Riston's lass. Robert, the boat man."

"Boat man?" Noah blinks again and swipes a fine drool from his chin on the sleeve of his doublet. His grip loosens.

"Witch, indeed," roars Amos, thundering up the path. He looms over me.

I will not let him know I'm afraid. I will not. He is so close I smell stale sweat and spilled food caked upon his doublet. And I can see every rotten yellow tooth in his mouth when he leers into my face. He binds my wrists, picks me up off the ground, and sets me on my feet. Then he clips me about the head and shoulders, knocking me down again. My head spins and I fear I will scream with pain.

"Your turn now, Noah," he says. "Tether the witch."

Noah binds a rope around my neck as he is bid, and they drag me back to the Mullin cottage for all the world as if I were Hannah's milk cow.

Amos pushes me over the threshold. Master Mullin and the minister are on their knees, attempting to light a fire.

"Pa, look what Noah did find," shouts Amos.

Master Mullin spins around. "At last." He circles me like Samuel's dog herding sheep. At any moment I fear Master Mullin might nip my heels.

"This is the pale one, sure enough, Minister Jessey," crows Master Mullin.

The minister struggles to his feet and trips toward me clutching his pointy black hat upon his head. He reaches for a lock of my hair, for it must resemble hoarfrost in the gloomy light, but I glare into his moist, bloodshot eyes, and he lets drop his hand. All bombast and bluster, methinks.

"Amos, go quick and fetch the Goody family and Bramwell family from Cricklade," orders Master Mullin. "Inform them Minister Jessey will read the grievance list against the pale one tomorrow. Soon we will be done with this witch once and for all."

chapter *sixteen*

Noah is commanded to remove me into the barn for safekeeping. But he thinks to rid me of the rope about my neck before nudging me onto the pile of hay where the satchel containing my pathetic collection of goods is still hid. And all at once the slow beginning of a scheme to save my own life picks and pecks in my brain.

"What think you, Noah? Might I escape this place?"

He shuffles across the dusty floor, past the byre where Hannah milked her cow, and hunches by the barn door the better to keep watch over me. Night has fallen fast, but moonlight shines bright through the cracks in the roof.

"Do you hear me?" I call. With my hands still bound it is a difficult task to struggle from the haystack, but somehow I hasten to his side. "Do you?"

"You killed my ma," he slobbers into his sleeve.

"Noah, I did not. She died of the plague. After you left, many more in the village succumbed."

Noah scratches his head. "Pa said was your witchy ways," he mumbles.

I squat beside him. "Noah, Hannah did not think me a witch. She told me so. Surely you do not think Hannah mistaken? You need to think for yourself."

He buries his head between his knees so I can scarce make out a word he says. "Cannot," he sputters.

"Cannot what, Noah?"

"Think. Pa says I were born daft 'cause your ma fixed a hex on my ma."

I gaze at Hannah's slow-witted brother and begin to feel sorry for his miserable life. Sorry he must endure a bully for a father and a brute for a brother.

"And what did your sister Hannah say?" I whisper.

Noah shakes his head back and forth like the Ting-Tang bell. His tiny eyes gleam. "That I were a good boy," he gulps.

"Hannah would tell you to be a good boy now and untie my hands." I hold my breath. Will he do it? Will he help me? "Please, Noah."

He snuffles into his sleeve.

"Hannah would want it."

"Hannah." Noah sways onto his bandy legs and struggles with the knots, which Amos bound uncommon tight. Red welts adorn my wrists, and I yearn for a fomentation of chamomile flowers to ease the inflammation. Noah dabs at my sores with stubby fingers. "Hannah is gone."

"Yes, Hannah is gone."

It is only days ago that Hannah died in Jack's arms. It is hard to accept that I could do naught to save her but harder yet to accept that Jack abandoned me. Threatened me. And willfully took his own life.

"Noah, do you want to know the whereabouts of Hannah?"

Noah nods.

"Then you must help me."

His shoulders slump. "Pa'll whip me."

"He does not have to know. It can be our secret. Just you and me."

"Secret?" His wooden face cracks into a wobbly smile. "Hannah and me had a secret."

"What was that Noah?"

"She was sweet on Jack Marlow."

"She was, Noah, she was that." I take his face in my hands. "Listen, Noah, tomorrow your pa and Minister Jessey plan to brand me a witch and float me in the river. I must flee, but I need your help."

Noah is silent.

I retreat to the mound of hay and retrieve my satchel. "Will you take this to St. John's Bridge for me?" I ask, holding out the bag toward him.

Noah frowns. Does he fathom what I need of him?

"I promise to stay in the barn. I won't get you into trouble."

How best to reach into his thick head and persuade him to aid me? I nudge him aside and heave open the barn door. No candles burn in the Mullin cottage. Pray God Master Mullin and the minister sleep soundly.

I whistle softly. And whistle again. Wings swoosh from the spinney through the frosty air, and soon my white bird struts through the doorway. Noah scuffles away from us, bewildered gasps popping from his slack, slobbering jaw.

"Stay, Noah." But still he shambles backward, tripping on Hannah's abandoned milk stool. "Stand still. Be a good boy. Hannah said you were a good boy."

"Hannah?" Noah gurgles. "Hannah."

But he heeds me, transfixed by my beautiful bird. She dances on the dusty floor. Her claws scritch scratch amongst pieces of dry hay and cracked seed. She pecks Noah's boots and caws deep in her throat. Noah chuckles.

"Hold out your hand." I pluck my rook from the floor and place her in Noah's huge fist. She preens and primps her snow-white feathers. Noah is absolutely still, happiness trickling slowly across his simple face.

"Noah, tomorrow if you do exactly what I ask of you, this noble bird will take you to Hannah."

I reach into the satchel for my knife and slip it between my skirt and pinny, for I shall need it to aid in my plan. Then I remember the rose petals in my pocket.

"When she does, give these to Hannah."

"Hannah?"

"Yes. For Hannah. A gift from Gwendoline Riston."

I wrench open the barn door once again, and my white rook soars into the chill darkness. If I can be rid of this place and these vengeful people tomorrow, I know I shall never set eyes upon my beautiful bird again.

She has been my guardian angel since Pappy hid me in the secret chamber. And she was my mammy's, too, carrying her soul safely up to heaven. But this loss I must bear, for the bird has served us well. And it is time for Noah to have an angel of his own, for Lord knows, without his sister to watch out for him, he is in great need of protection.

chapter *seventeen*

The day dawns frigid cold. A cold wind whistles through the chinks in the roof. Noah fetches me a beaker of water and a slice of bread from the cottage but does not look into my face.

"Noah, the satchel? Did you do as I bid?"

"Secret," he gurgles.

"Yes, Noah," I breathe. "We have a secret."

I place my carved wooden bird into his fist for the time has come for me to part with it. "She is yours now, Noah."

In a flash my treasure disappears into his doublet.

"Follow the bird till she alights, Noah. When you see Hannah's comb you will know her whereabouts."

Noah retrieves his rope and ties it around my waist before leading me outside the barn. Clouds grow grim and a snowflake

flutters from the lowering sky. If the weather worsens I will
freeze to death before I can escape the village. Minister Jessey,
Master Mullin, and Amos join us and together we tread from the
cottage to the green. Clustered there are the Goody family and
the Bramwell family, fetched by Amos back to Letchlade. And a
dozen or so more survivors trail up the lanes. Their clothing is
much worn. Their faces gaunt. They cringe, sullen and fearful at
the sight of me. Foolish dolts. Noah prods me onto the edge of
the trough, where I perch snug in my shawl. A rime of ice fringes
the water now.

All about me gather the ghosts of summer past: vindictive
Joe, combative Mistress Mullin, ill-fated Reverend Morton, love
besotted Hannah and Jack. But now Old Samuel, hunched over his
crook, hobbles onto the green. Not a ghost at all. His collie sidles
close. How soothing is the dog's wet tongue upon my hands.

Master Mullin faces the gathering. "Now you are assembled,
let us begin this proceeding without delay. Most of you will
remember that Reverend Morton refused to seek out the pale one
who did bewitch my wife," says Master Mullin. "He advised me to
seek justice elsewhere. So I did heed his word. I sold our passage
to the New World. And instead sought the services of Minister
Jessey in Burford who knows well what is necessary to prove a
case of witchcraft."

Minister Jessey lunges at me on his pointy toes, plucks my
cap from my head, and it is right away snatched skyward in a
gust of wind. "Look at her," he shrieks, as my hair furls about
my head. "Her pallor is otherworldly." He shakes a bony finger

at the folks assembled. "You all saw what this witch did do to Mistress Mullin?"

"Aye." They nod and mutter behind their hands.

He turns to me. "We know you were in the Church of St. Giles. For we found proof of your witchy ways." His voice rises to a squeak. "A circle of candles, communion wine poured in a most pagan way, vestments defiled."

Mistress Goody cries out in horror. Master Goody spits. His saliva clings to a single tress of my hair. I wince, my stomach roils. But I will not dignify his act by scrubbing it away.

"Where were you hid?" yelps Minister Jessey.

I shrug. I'll never tell. Never will I reveal the secret chamber to these ignorant fools. No one will know of it. Ever.

"She speaks not," he squeals. "Certain proof of guilt!"

"Waste no more time," orders Master Mullin, impatient to seek revenge. Determined to see me dead.

Minister Jessey pulls a scroll of parchment from his black cape. It crackles in the cold wind. Since neither I nor anyone else assembled can read the written word, it may contain abracadabras for all I know. He gathers himself up and clears his throat.

"Herewith, I read a list of grievances as were drawn up in Burford in the year of our Lord 1665 against one, Gwendoline Riston.

1. *That on the day of her birth a familiar was observed by Mistress Mullin on the roof of the cottage of Robert Riston, boatman of the village of Letchlade.*

2. *That said child was observed by Mistress Mullin floating in the*

river, clearly aided by the Devil in this most unnatural of acts.

3. *That said child disappeared into thin air this past summer and from an unknown hiding place did cause five hundred rooks to perch upon her cottage and later perish.*

4. *That said child did appear in apparition in the Church of St. Giles accompanied by her familiar in the form of a pure white rook and did strike said Mistress Mullin dead.*

5. *That said child did consort with the Devil in the shape of a rook for the purposes of casting spells and in so doing did cause the plague deaths of fifty persons in all.*

When he is done with the damning list there is a deep silence about the village green. And a familiar sour smell of fear hangs in the frigid autumn air, much as it did when Pappy tried to warn them of the plague. Even Master Mullin seems lost for words. Noah just scuffs his boots through the brittle grass. Noah has a secret to keep.

Then Samuel breaks the silence. "You come back here with the cold north winds and think to blame an innocent lass for your woes," he says to the villagers. "If you'd a-listened to Robert Riston the plague would have passed you by." His voice crackles with indignation. "None of this would of happened."

"Fie. Go bleat to your sheep, old man," shouts Master Bramwell. "What do you know of the ways of the world?"

"Enough to know Gwendoline Riston is no witch. This child is a healer."

Master Mullin lumbers toward him, but Samuel points a knotty finger. "I'll wager you had no thought to ask the whereabouts of the daughter you abandoned in your haste to seek vengeance," sneers Samuel. "Never sought to learn her fate."

At mention of Hannah, I dare not glance at Noah for fear he will give away our secret. But he is still.

A ruby red flush spreads from Master Mullin's ugly square neck to the top of his cropped head. "How dare you," he spits.

"I'll have ye know Gwendoline Riston tried with all her might to save your lass from the plague, long after all in the village had fled. She gave her shelter. She drained her swellings. She nursed her mortal sick body. . . ."

But with every detail, all in the crowd hiss like adders slithering through the gorse. Samuel's words cannot help because none knew that Hannah Mullin had found her way back to Letchlade. None knew her fate. Now they draw close and the menace in their eyes drips like venom. I must act quickly.

"Let me prove this dispute once and for all," I shout. "Throw me in the river. If I float I am a witch. If I sink I am cleared of your grievous accusations!"

Before I can catch a breath, Master Mullin catches the rope about my waist, just as I hoped. Past the tavern, through the churchyard, and across the meadow to the river I am dragged, trailed by the jeering villagers.

And all the time I think of the fearsome hot summer evenings I waited for Pappy on the riverbank. Particularly I fix in my mind the willow by the first river bend that sweeps the surface of the water like a giant broom.

But now the wind is chill and ripples the surface of the water.

"Gwendoline Riston, at your own request we prove now whether you be a witch," squawks Minister Jessey. His cape snaps in the wind. Mucous drips from the end of his pointy nose.

"Aye," I reply, "and since you be an expert on witchery, I do also request that you hold the rope that will prove which one of us is right!" I stare at Minister Jessey again, as I did upon our first meeting in the Mullin cottage. "For if I float you will have the satisfaction of pulling a witch from the river. And if I be innocent you can haul my body from the water and give me a Christian burial."

Minister Jessey quakes. But he accepts the rope from Master Mullin. "Surely, you are not afraid," I taunt. "You, a man of God."

Do my mist gray eyes and powdery lashes disturb him? Does my pallid complexion cause him fear? Uncertainty sits upon his pinched, mean face.

"And let Noah Mullin bind me," I shout, "for it was he discovered my whereabouts."

The crowd is mute now, waiting in the frigid morning air to see if the pale one sinks or swims. Master Mullin tosses a short hank of rope to Noah.

"Lash it loose, Noah," I breathe beneath the soughing of the trees, "and the white bird will lead you to Hannah's resting place."

Through Noah's sour smell I detect the faint scent of rose petals. Praise be, he still carries my gift for Hannah.

"Get on with it, halfwit," mutters Amos. "Else I'll do it for you."

Noah presses upon my back to bend me double in preparation for the ordeal. He tosses aside my clogs in order to bind left thumb to right toe, then right thumb to left toe in the form of the holy cross.

It has always seemed to me a forgiving God would not condone such abuse of the crucifix.

When Noah lifts me in his arms and trudges to the river's edge I draw breath best I can in my contorted position. It needs be the deepest breath I have ever drawn if I am to survive.

"Secret," Noah mumbles.

Then he casts me into the air. I arc high about the river like a crescent moon. If all else fails at least the water will cleanse Master Goody's spit from my hair. I hit the biting cold water with a mighty splash.

chapter eighteen

I have only moments to slip from Noah's knots before reaching the bottom of the river. I wiggle my fingers and toes. Thank God the bindings slip away like wax down a candle. Simple Noah served me well.

Desperate am I for a handhold on the riverbed that will prevent me bouncing to the surface. Careful not to disturb the mud and so alert the watchers to my whereabouts, I search the river bottom with the palms of my hands: smooth stones, slippery grasses, shoals of silver minnow.

At last! A tree root! It is anchored well in the sludge, and I hold on tight with my left hand. But I had not reckoned on how to slice the rope with the use of only one hand! I fix the rope that attaches me to Minister Jessey between my knees and tug the knife from my waist. I start to hack, all the time holding my breath. When I fear my wrists will snap in two, the final threads of rope fray. I grab the end of the rope before it can slack, let the knife slip from my hand, and loop the rope around the tree root.

Next I shrug off my shawl and squirm from my skirt, the better to use my arms and legs. When I have wriggled from these cumbersome clothes and wear naught but a shift, I flip upon my belly.

Already my chest burns for lack of air. With wide-open eyes, I flick and flip much as my fish do toward the overhanging willow at the first river bend. Trout tickle my cheeks. Sticklebacks dart through my hair. But my limbs weaken. I am dizzy now in the head.

At last my head breaks the surface and I release my breath. The Lord is with me, for I find myself well hid beneath the willow fronds. I cling to the trunk, shuddering with cold, and gulp the bitter-cold air till my head stops spinning and my lungs stop stinging.

Upstream, angry voices clamor across the water meadows.

"Pull her out, pull her out!" shouts Master Mullin. "She's been in the river long enough."

"Let us see if she be dead or alive," yells Amos.

"I can scarce believe her innocent," complains Master Bramwell.

And then a hush descends. Not a sound can I hear, not a bird in the sky, not a squirrel scampering up an oak tree. All is hushed.

I tweak the fronds to peep. And what I see pleases me well. Minister Jessey hovers on pointy toes, dangling a length of empty rope. Neither a witch nor an innocent does he reel in. Nothing. Nothing at all.

Then the mob rallies. They thrash in the weeds and hurl stones in the river, wanting vengeance. Wanting evidence of a broken body. Up and down the banks they stomp, cursing and swearing. Master Goody hoists my skirt from the churned-up river on the end of a stick. Mistress Goody discovers my shawl tangled in reeds. But nowhere do they find their witch.

My breath is steady once more and the pain in my lungs abated, although I fear my fingers and toes numb fast. But I must put distance between the mob and myself and retrieve my clothing, else perish of cold in a very short time.

I reckon it is close to midday when I clamber from the river. It is far colder out of the water wearing naught but my wet shift. My hair cascades down my back in sodden ringlets. Pray no one is about to spy me in such a state.

Shivering mightily I scour beneath St. John's Bridge for my satchel, to no avail. I search the hedgerows about the bridge. I explore the riverbank up and down, but no bag can I find. I am colder by the minute, and my limbs grow steadily hard and stiff, making it difficult to move. In desperation, I climb the bank and struggle across the span of the bridge, risking exposure to any villagers who might be searching for me.

I can scarce believe my luck. There, in the middle of the bridge for all to see, is the satchel, delivered by Noah. It has been there since last evening and all of today, and not a soul has touched it—a miracle indeed.

Much cheered, I seek the protection of a clump of gorse and shed my sodden shift. I dress quickly, thinking to don both wool

skirts, two shifts, both blouses and bodice, before bundling myself into my warm cloak. Please God, let these layers melt the chill
and thaw my bones. I chafe my arms and legs and then the tips
of my ears and the length of my nose until blood begins to flow
through my body once more.

To my utter amazement I discover beneath the clothing in
my satchel a loaf of bread, three strips of salted eel, and two
wizened apples. Tears flow, for Noah is not such a dullard as
I believed. He possesses much kindness and a gentle nature
lodged inside a damaged body. Indeed, I took advantage of
Noah to save myself and take little pride in it. But if the bird
guides Noah safe to Hannah's resting place and watches over
him as he travels this life, I can think of no better way to bestow
my thanks.

Aching with loneliness I sup a handful of water and watch the
river flowing over moss-covered rocks, between reed and bulrush,
through water meadows, beckoning me forward. For I must heed
Pappy's advice to find Lord Bathurst and beg his protection. Somehow I must gather the strength to follow this river all the way to
Hampton Court.

I sleep soundly beneath the stone bridge but wake to a drub-
bing sleet. While I wait for the squall to pass I gobble up a portion
of Noah's bread with a strip of eel. The remaining vittles I stash
in the folds of my cloak. My clothing is upon my person. All the
satchel contains now is the half-knitted pair of hose I struggled
to make for Jack. I hurl the satchel and its contents into the river
and watch it sink slowly into the silt.

A bitter wind blows and I must not tarry. I pull my hood tight about my head and set forth barefoot down the towpath. How I miss the clogs Noah cast aside when he trussed me for the floating.

I follow the winding towpath eastward, hardly daring to think how many miles I must travel to reach Hampton Court. It is very far beyond Oxford, closer, I believe, to the city of London.

No fresh piles of manure dot the overgrown track. No horse has pulled a barge this far upstream for some long time. Nettle patches sprout in abundance. Beyond the water meadows neglected fields are choked with dock and sorrel.

My feet are soon swollen and blood oozes from cuts and scratches, but somehow I manage to struggle on for six whole days, resting at night along the river bank. I try to eke out my small supply of food, but try as I might it is soon finished and I find little to forage along the way except shriveled blackberries and a few wild onion in the hedgerows.

On the seventh day of my journey I observe a frayed length of rope upon the path, a discarded wheelbarrow, and then a willow basket rattling back and forth in the icy wind. Clearly folk have passed this way. Pray God I will meet someone up ahead to aid me, for my limbs ache badly, and my torn feet worse still.

Shortly thereafter, as I stumble along the towpath in a shower of sleet, I come upon a row of moored barges. But the silence is eerie. Not a tethered horse do I glimpse, not a boatman, not even a mongrel dog.

"Greetings," I call, upon reaching the first boat. "Is anyone there?" But no one responds.

The second boat I clearly recognize as the London barge that carried the gentry to Letchlade. Odd bits of finery spill from looted trunks. What has become of these fancy folk? Do their bodies rot below deck?

Horrified, I struggle down the path to the next boat, and the next, and the next. Frozen raindrops sting my lips and cling to my cheeks. When I lurch around a wide bend in the river, one last barge is moored to the bank. It seems as deserted as the rest, but if any strength remained in my body I would cry out to the heavens. For I know this boat and its discovery causes the blood to pound through my veins.

chapter nineteen

I stumble onto Pappy's boat deck and reel across the planks on bloodied feet. Buckets are overturned, ropes tangled, and shreds of fleece cling to the boards. But nowhere is there sight nor sound of Pappy himself, only the splish splash of the river against the boat as it rocks side to side.

Breathing deeply to stay my trembling limbs, I grasp the worn railing, bleached and blistered by the searing sun of last summer and force myself down the ladder into the dim cabin. A loaf, blackened with age, rolls across the floor. Mold sprouts from a round of cheese upon the table. Pappy's stool is overturned, one leg broken off. The mattress is shredded. Goose feathers overflow the floor and flutter in the fusty air like snowflakes. But there is no dead body.

I hardly know if I need laugh or cry. If the plague took Pappy would there not be his remains? It seems more probable a gang of knaves raided the boat some while ago. Searching for booty, sovereigns and the like, earned from the wool trade. Pray Pappy had abandoned the barge before this time and set off with Rosie to seek Jack in Oxford.

It is still daylight, but I collapse upon the bunk and fall into an exhausted slumber. Despite the lack of soft bedding 'tis well to have a roof above my head after nights spent sleeping on the riverbank. When I wake next morning and peek through the porthole, the distant wolds are veiled in snow. A kingfisher skims the water in a flash of blue. Cows low in a distance meadow. A kestrel cries in the slate gray sky.

My plight is desperate. My feet are so swelled I cannot bear weight upon them. I have no food. After all I have suffered I fear my life will shortly sap away as surely as autumn spins to winter.

I sink lower in Pappy's bunk and let myself be rocked like a babby in its cradle by the lapping river. I fade into a netherworld. Dream fragments torment me: Hannah's ravaged body upon her deathbed; the sharp smell of gunpowder upon the wolds; the slam of wet soil upon the earthly remains of Hannah and Jack.

Then in the midst of my nightmares a tinkling bell rouses me. I struggle onto an elbow and peer out the window. Nothing do I see but my swift-running river and crusts of hoar frost upon the towpath. I pitch back upon the bunk. But I hear it again, a faint plink. Somehow I totter to the ladder and some-

how I heave myself onto the deck. Again and again I hear
faraway bells.

Sullen clouds smear the heavens. The bells chime again. I clamber off the barge, bind my cloak close, and lurch down the towpath.

My ears hearken to a well-known rasping tread scraping the
frosty ground. Yes! I am sure of it now, despite I can see naught,
for the river still winds in its loops and bends through the wide,
flat fields. The uneven gait grows louder. The chink of bells grows
closer. I stumble onward, gasping in pain, praying to God I am
not deceived.

And around the next turn there is my reward. For dear Rosie,
harness bells a-jingle, plods slowly toward me on massive hooves.
And best of all she is led by the hulking brawn of the dearest man
in all the world, his long gray hair swept back in its pigtail beneath
the familiar floppy felt hat.

Such a bleak sadness drains from my soul. "Pappy, oh Pappy,
you are alive," I cry, but my frail voice is naught but a whisper. My
words fritter away on the frigid wind.

Then my legs buckle. I crumple to the ground like a sack of
kindling, for I am frozen stiff, my bones brittle cold, and my feet
so puffed I can stagger no farther.

When I open my eyes Pappy is knelt before me, sprinkling
water upon my brow. And Rosie blows air from her nostrils
about my face and neck and licks my damaged feet with her
thick pink tongue.

"She does thaw you out and warm you up, my angel here on
earth girl. I can scarce believe it's you." Pappy kisses my forehead

and sweeps me into his arms. On his doublet is the faint but treasured odor of fresh-sheared fleece and damp river pastures. How blessed sweet this is to me.

"I so feared that you were dead," I murmur.

"Nay, child, but I have been trapped in Oxford till this very morn when the plague threat was deemed over. I set out to seek you without delay, but it seems it is you who found me." Pappy gazes at me in wonder. "It is hard to trust my own eyes. My only consolation was that you were safe in the secret chamber."

"I was. The villagers died or fled the plague just as you predicted." I shudder. "But Pappy, when I ventured forth, I was captured by Master Mullin and accused of witchcraft. They tossed me in the river." I finally allow myself to weep at the horror of it all. "But I did escape and set forth to seek Lord Bathurst as you instructed."

"And you do not have so far to go," Pappy whispers, lifting me onto Rosie's warm back. "He and his family are but three miles hence with the King in Oxford Castle."

"Only three more miles," I gasp, weaving my fingers through Rosie's thick mane. "How easily we might have missed each other for I was seeking Lord Bathurst at Hampton Court."

"Parliament left there and sought sanctuary in Oxford from the plague," Pappy explains. "Where Parliament goes, so goes the King."

"Are we safe now, Pappy? Please tell me we are, for I can bear no more."

"Indeed we are. Lord Bathurst does not forget his debt. He even now restores the Manor House for his family. And we are promised shelter for as long as we live."

"'Tis just as well," I whisper, "for our cottage was burned to the ground." I cling to Rosie's neck for comfort. "The villagers turned against us."

Pappy's blue eyes shimmer. "Just as they abandoned Lady Bathurst when Cromwell's louts tried to destroy the Manor House." Pappy blinks. "But before all else let me tend your ills." He pulls a thick wedge of brown bread from his saddlebag. "Eat slow, angel here on earth girl," he warns, "for there will be precious little room in that shrunken belly of yours."

I let each morsel melt on my tongue. Nothing in all my life tasted so well.

"Do you know anything of Jack's whereabouts?" he asks suddenly, his brow creased with dread. "He and his master were fled from Oxford before my return."

I stare at the distant snow-clad wolds where Jack deliberately ended his life. I cannot speak this awful truth. For it would break poor Pappy's heart to learn how Jack threatened me. And then forsook us.

"Jack returned to the village in search of Hannah Mullin. He was much smitten—"

"Yes, I suspected as much," Pappy mutters.

"Hannah died of the plague. I tried with all my might to save her—"

"And Jack, too? Did he succumb?"

I nod.

"So both are gone from this world?" he chokes.

I nod again.

"I feared this end." Pappy's face is wracked with sorrow. "This plague has wrought such desperate devastation."

I lean past Rosie's neck and rest my head on Pappy's shoulder. "I am sorry that I could not save Jack for you," I weep. "For like you I loved him with all my heart."

"My angel here on earth girl, what miseries you have endured, but we must thank the good Savior we have found each other once again. And we must tarry not, for the weather turns." Pappy lifts his face to the ominous sky and sniffs. "There is snow in the air, I am sure of it."

He clambers behind me onto Rosie's broad back and guides her from the towpath, across a pasture, and onto a wide cart track. "'Tis the Oxford Road," he explains. "We will return to Court and inform Lord Bathurst of your survival."

The road is clogged with carrier carts, laden with hay, firewood, and animal carcasses. "Word spreads fast that the city is open once more," says Pappy. "Trade will be brisk by nightfall."

Wagon wheels grind through the frozen ruts, and I cover my ears at the din. Carters shout greetings, oaths, and curses one to another. Hawkers line the road offering trinkets and sweetmeats to passing coaches. I care not for this stink and noise and confusion. But Rosie plods steadily on as calm as if she were alone upon the riverbank.

"The city is close now," says Pappy.

And soon enough we clop over a stone bridge and clatter up a steep cobbled way. Ahead of us looms the castle with dank walls smudged with soot, four gaunt, gray towers studded with arrow slips, and a drawbridge spanning a dry moat.

Rosie trots into an enormous courtyard, flanked by the western tower wall, stables, coach houses, and what smells much like a brewery. Scullery maids scuttle about the cobblestones hefting buckets of water from the pump, and grooms heave mountains of manure into piles beyond the stables.

Pappy lifts me from Rosie's back, hands her reins to a stable lad, and carries me in his arms across the yard into a cavernous kitchen. The air is heavy with the mingled odors of succulent roasts, sour blood, ripe fruit, and baking bread. Never have I imagined so much food in one place in my life.

Clutching me to his chest, Pappy treads up a gloomy, winding stairwell. The steps open upon a paradise: rugs strewn on stone floors, walls lined with tapestries, sills filled with bouquets of pot pourri, and window frames hung with pomander balls.

Pappy lowers me gently to the floor and my swollen feet sink into a thick woven carpet. "This way to his Lordship's apartment." He guides me along a corridor, through an arched doorway, and into a chamber, thick with a fug of smoke.

"Riston! You are quickly returned from your quest," mutters a stout fellow sucking hard on a long clay pipe. He is sat beside the fire near a square table covered with a red-flocked cloth that drapes clear to the floor. Upon the table are a pile of books, rolls of parchment, and pots of ink. A young man scribbles away with a quill pen, oblivious to our presence.

"I discovered Gwendoline along the towpath," Pappy explains, nudging me forward. I struggle to curtsey best I can. "Sadly, milord, she brings word that my dear Jack has perished."

"I am sorry, Robert. Truly sorry. This is tragic news in - deed." Lord Bathurst rises from his chair, his face etched with concern. "I know you considered him a true son." His eyes fall on the youth intent upon his work. "If it were my son Lawrence who had died I should be devastated as well you know."

At the mention of his name the young man rises from the table, knocking over an inkwell in his haste. He blushes clear to his toes when he sets eyes upon me. And indeed, what a sight I must present, still wearing each item of clothing I possess, one atop the other, all ripped and torn and stained with muck. And from beneath my skirts protrude my bloody, bloated feet.

"We will feed and clothe you shortly," Lord Bathurst declares, turning his attention to me. But as he speaks a door beyond the fireplace swings open with a gush of cold air.

"Edward, we will feed and clothe her this instant," declares Lady Bathurst sweeping into the room, for it can be no other to address his Lordship such. "Have you no consideration for the girl's needs?"

"I intended only to inquire briefly of what has transpired in our village these past several months," protests Lord Bathurst.

Lady Bathurst glides across the carpet, skirts all a-swish. "There will be time enough for that, Edward."

She presses me into her ample bosom, her velvet gown as soft as eiderdown and smelling sweetly of lavender, and I imagine this might be how a mother holds a daughter. Lady Bathurst strokes my hair with a smooth and slender hand. "Indeed, you are your mother's child and no other," she whispers in my ear. "She was a wondrous woman indeed."

I glance again at the youth called Lawrence, who is clumsily trying to mop up the flood of ink seeping into the red cloth, and simultaneously trying to move his multitude of books to the floor before they are stained. He is short like his father. His strong square face is clean-shaven; his dark hair is pulled away from a jutting jaw; his bright brown eyes shine behind spectacles perched upon a thin straight nose. Methinks how quite unlike Jack he seems in every conceivable way.

Before I can draw breath Lady Bathurst has whisked me away to Pappy's room. A copper tub is set before the fire, and a parade of serving wenches fill it with pitchers of boiling water. Her Ladyship peels each article of clothing from my body until they are piled in a filthy heap upon the floor.

"Now you must soothe away those aches and pains, Gwendoline," she says, sprinkling a handful of sweet-smelling herbs into the tub.

And grateful I am to slip into the steamy water and soak myself clean. "You are too kind," I whisper.

Lady Bathurst fixes me with her big brown eyes. "Nay, I owe your mother much, Gwendoline. When you father hid me in that secret chamber, it was she who healed me, for I was at great risk of losing the babe in my belly."

"Lawrence was that babby?"

"He was indeed." Lady Bathurst nods. "Only your dear mother knew what concoction would stave off the pains. And keep me safe till I reached full term."

But I cannot think on it now, for a great drowsiness overcomes me. I am shortly wrapped in a thick robe, sat before the fire, fed a porringer of sweet bread soaked in milk and honey, and tucked between crisp linen sheets for the night.

chapter *twenty*

When I wake the next morn Lady Bathurst has laid out for me a fine wool skirt, blouse, bodice, and shawl. But most special are a pair of red satin slip-shoes that shimmer and sparkle in the winter light streaming through the casement. Such fancies!

When I am refreshed and fed and the glorious slippers adorn my feet, Pappy declares he will show me every nook and cranny of this great castle whilst Lord Bathurst attends the King.

As we proceed down a wide corridor I keep watch upon the floor for a glimpse of a shining red toe each time one peeks from beneath my skirt. So intent am I upon my finery I do not immediately notice a gaggle of small dogs that burst beneath an archway. They scamper across the sumptuous carpet and so un-resemble Samuel's collie that I burst out laughing. Not one burr-tangled, mud-spattered coat amongst them, only straight silken fur sweeping the rug as they frolic to and fro.

Striding in their wake is the tallest man I have ever set eyes upon. Long Cavalier curls fly about his face, a thin mustache graces his upper lip, and he drips velvet and lace.

"Kneel, Gwen-child," urges Pappy. "'Tis the King of England!"

Gathered behind the monarch is an entourage of courtiers. Their cloying scents waft about the hallway and tickle my nose till I sneeze. Behind them all I spy young Lawrence looking most discomforted. Methinks he wishes himself anywhere but with this gathering for he appears to be much more a scholar than a dandy.

As I sink to the floor one little dog escapes its companions and burrows into my lap, like a mole seeking sanctuary from the light. Head bowed, I caress her silky fur and marvel at the softness of her coat.

His Majesty draws close, calling his dogs to heel, but the little one heeds him not. I gently coax her to return to her king but still she stays close to me, her heart pounding against my thigh. From my position on the floor I view silver buckles on high-heeled shoes and handsome calves clad in black hose.

"Who is this lily white maid that so beguiles my pet?"

Lord Bathurst comes to my rescue. "She is the daughter of Riston, Sire."

"Riston?"

"You will recall, Sire, that Riston did save my wealth and my family from Oliver Cromwell's soldiers. He has been with us at Court for the duration."

Pappy limps across the floor and stoops low. "Though my daughter was hid from the plague, I feared greatly for her life, Sire. Praise be to God I have found her—"

"Yes, yes," the King interrupts with a wave of his hand.

The dogs tumble about, yipping and barking and chasing their tails, all but the poor creature that trembles in the folds of my skirt. "What ails thee, little creature of God?" I murmur into her silken ear, for she whimpers in a most distressed manner.

"What indeed," roars King Charles, taking heed of me once more. "She pants and paces my chamber all night and drives Lady Wyckham to distraction."

"*And* she makes a fair stink," declares a bold beauty, whom I assume to be Lady Wyckham herself.

"Be silent, wench," cries the King.

"You needs choose, Sire," she retorts, sweeping to the ground in a deep curtsey. "'Tis me or this farting dog, for there is not room for the two of us in your bedchamber!"

The entire entourage erupts in laughter at her sauce. I dare to glance upward. Two angry red spots adorn the King's cheeks. "Well, little maid, the dog seems loath to leave you. What do you propose we do now?"

My fingers explore the distended belly of the poor beast. It is clear she is plugged tight as a barrel of ale and in much discomfort. She wriggles and squirms and pushes her brown and white domed head into my belly, desperate for relief.

Pappy crouches beside me on the carpet. "Can you heal her?" he breathes.

Aghast, I shake my head. "I could not save Hannah from the plague," I whisper. "I have no more wish to concoct salves and potions."

I cannot help but recall the one who blamed me for Hannah Mullin's death. Jack's cruel words hiss and spit in my head, and an unbidden tear splashes upon my bodice.

"Oh, angel here on earth girl," Pappy chides. "Why—"

"No physician in the land can cure the plague, child," interrupts Lord Bathurst, looming over Pappy and me. "Heaven knows, many have tried."

"His Lordship is right," whispers Pappy. "But take pity on this poor creature, for you can ease her pain, I am sure of it."

But I am frozen with fear. How I wish to disappear from this place. All about me the fancy ladies swirl their voluptuous skirts, flash their wanton eyes, whisper behind their fans.

"Well, maid, answer your King. What ails my pup?"

I rise to my feet, not daring to look into the face of my monarch. If I try to help but fail, can he chop off my head? Or lock me in the Tower of London?

"I await your answer, maid."

"She is much obstructed," I murmur. "But it is late autumn and bitter cold. No remedy will be at hand this time of year, so I cannot—"

"Is there not a still-room in this confounded castle?" the King bellows. "Will someone not take this maid at once, that she can cure my dog?"

There is a sudden commotion as Lawrence nudges his way through the throng of courtiers and sweeps into a bow before the King, his face all a-flush.

"I will aid the lass, Sire, for I am well acquainted with the still-room."

So it seems I have no choice but to do my best to ease the pup's condition. For I cannot refuse the wishes of the King of England!

"Bring her to the banquet one day hence," says King Charles, "after which I depart this dreary place for pleasures elsewhere."

The king swivels away from me on his shiny black shoes to grasp the arm of Lady Wyckham. "Beware, Madam," he bellows, his face close to hers. "I'll not be bested by a dog. Nor, Madam, will I be bested by you!" The entourage again erupts into laughter as they move down the halls.

And so I am left in charge of the king's pup with only a day to affect a purge! Lawrence guides me down corridors and stairways, through the enormous kitchen, and into a cool, whitewashed still-room next the dairy.

Never have I imagined so many bottles and potions in one place: jars of ointments, bottles of roots, boxes of bark and berries, all arrayed on shelf after shelf, enough to overwhelm me.

"How is it that you are familiar with this place?" I ask, cradling the pup in my arms. "Seems an unlikely place for the son of a Lord to inhabit."

"And what should the son of a Lord be about?" Lawrence asks, his spectacles sliding down his nose.

"I had not thought," I mumble. "I do not intend any impertinence."

"And I do not take it so." Lawrence blushes. "I make a study of medicine at the university," he explains. "I am particularly interested in the healing properties of plants." His arms sweep about the shelves and the dried flowers and herbs hanging from the ceiling. "My parents tell me that your mother had a great know-ledge of such things. I understand that you inherited her gift?"

I do not respond. I failed to keep Hannah Mullin alive. Yet I do not know if my mammy would have succeeded under such circumstances. Regardless, Hannah's death hangs heavy on me.

"How might you fix the pup?" Lawrence asks. "For I wish to be of help."

In truth, I have no idea, except that once Hannah's milk cow had munched upon a bright pink spindle berry fallen on the ground, which caused the dung in her body to explode forth with such ferocity she was weakened for many weeks afterward. Spindle berries contain four black seeds each, wrapped in orange pulp. But which caused Hannah's cow to almost die? The seed? Or the pulp? Which was the poison? Which the purgative?

"Can you find me a berry from the spindle tree?" I ask.

I follow behind Lawrence as he searches the rows of jars. His stubby forefinger, stained with black ink, runs over each container as he reads the words written upon each. Finally he opens a jar. Inside are several bright pink berries. I sniff and know by the aroma that he has chosen correctly. But which part of the berry will purge the little dog without caus-ing harm?

Lawrence watches me intently as I remove a single berry from the jar and place it on a platter. I slice it open and remove the four black seeds. I scrape the dried orange pulp onto another platter.

"I need your help more, Lawrence. Can you fetch me some cheese from the kitchen?"

He is quickly returned with a wedge of golden yellow cheese. I cut four portions, slit each with my thumb nail, slip a black spindle seed into each cavity, and place all safely in the pocket of my new skirt.

"Now what we need are some handy rat holes."

I settle the King's pup in a corner of the still-room. Lawrence follows me across the courtyard toward the kitchens from whence scraps of offal are tossed away, morning, noon, and night. I skirt the drab gray western wall. And sure enough there lie telltale rat droppings beneath narrow cavities in the slabs of stone. I place the four pieces of baited cheese a few inches from their lairs.

"We need to wait," I whisper.

"Then you must borrow this." Lawrence shrugs out of his cape and wraps it about my shoulders. It smells of dried parchment. Rich and earthy.

But we do not wait long. A snout appears between the blocks of stone. Then another and another. Whiskers twitch. Paws scrabble. Bald undulating tails slither on the cold cobbles. The wretched rodents snatch the cheese and sit boldly upon their haunches to devour the morsels with long yellow teeth.

Lawrence's eyes grow huge behind his spectacles. In truth, never have I seen a poison work so fast. The creatures jerk. And convulse. Then slump on the cobblestones, dead within seconds. Does seem Hannah's cow survived because she ate only one berry and was considerably larger than these rats.

"There lies my answer. The seeds are poisonous, so it stands to reason the pulp is what I seek."

Back in the warmth of the still-room, I grind the dry orange pulp with pestle and mortar until it is a fine powder.

"Let me fetch meat from the kitchen," offers Lawrence. "For without some tasty scraps, the pup will surely not sup her medicine."

It is a fine and sensible suggestion, for when Lawrence returns with a platter of boiled chicken, I chop up a spoonful, sprinkle it with spindle powder, and easily feed it to the pup. "This will aid you, little creature of God."

"I beg you let me make notes of all that you have done this day," says Lawrence. "For this knowledge deserves to be documented."

"Does it?" I mutter. "There are some call it witchcraft."

"But that is absurd."

"You do not know that I was tried for a witch?" My voice is quiet.

Lawrence's cheeks flame. He reaches an ink-stained hand toward me, but it trembles so, he must push it into a pocket. "What you have is a gift. Not a curse."

"Whether 'tis or not"—I shrug, embarrassed—"we must see to this pup."

Dusk falls. Snowflakes drift from the glum sky. The pup follows us outside to drink at the pump. I romp with her around the courtyard despite the cold and my painful sore feet. "Methinks she needs to frisk upon the wolds," I laugh. "Not waste her life in carriages and castles with a king."

"I too long for that," sighs Lawrence, as he watches the playful pup. "I do detest this wasteful life. But as soon as the King leaves Oxford I can complete my study at the university."

"And then after that must you attend Court?" I ask.

Lawrence shakes his head, and his eyes meet mine. "King Charles repays Papa's loyalty by allowing our family to return to Letchlade. When I have learned all I can here in Oxford I will join Papa and Mama and continue my research into the healing properties of plants. Particularly those that grow on the wolds."

All about us the flakes fall faster. Pup slurps more water and capers about my dazzling red slip-shoes.

Lawrence chuckles. "They do look like rubies fresh scattered in the snow. Fair fit for a queen, in my opinion."

For a moment or two a memory of Jack and I playing Kings and Queens in the secret chamber vexes my mind. But in truth, how very far away and long ago it all seems now. And I feel the leaden weight that is my heart shift and ease inside my chest.

Finally pup stops her cavorting about my shoes, sniffs hither and thither, squats upon the snow-covered cobbles, and releases the first poupen.

"Halleluiah, little creature of God," I cry. "You do toot your horn well!"

"Praise be to God, she is cured." Lawrence claps his hands.

And we both burst out laughing.

chapter *twenty-one*

"Come, my angel here on earth girl, for tonight we must attend the King." Pappy hugs me close before nestling the pup safe in the folds of my shawl. "But tomorrow we travel home with his Lordship's entourage to begin our lives anew under his full protection."

The vast banqueting hall is lit with flaming torches thrust into iron brackets. I breathe deep the sweet smoky smell of apple wood. The walls are hung with plump purple curtains to stay the winter winds, which whistle through the cracks, whittle beneath doors, wheedle round casement windows.

Pappy joins Lord and Lady Bathurst who are seated at the King's table, but Lawrence is not yet in attendance. Perhaps he is so intent on some puzzling property of a certain plant that he forgets the time. Certain sure, Lawrence Bathurst is a book-worm and I like the notion well.

I linger in the shadows close by the vast arched doorway, hoping that His Majesty might overlook my presence and forget his pup, for I am already much attached. "Precious creature of God," I croon, kissing the tip of her black nose, "I shall miss your company sore." I am rewarded with a long lazy lick upon my cheek.

Fine ladies balance glossy wigs upon their heads, juggle bosoms that tumble from their gowns, and jostle for seats nearest their king. Queen Catherine is sat upon her husband's right, and a beautiful and sad lady she does seem.

So intent am I on this dazzling scene that I almost jump from my skin when Lawrence tumbles through the doorway pulling on a velvet doublet. He too is startled to see me there, especially because his jacket is all in a twist and he is muttering and curs-ing at his cumbersome finery. He grins guiltily as he tidies his doublet and sets straight his spectacles upon his nose. Then he pulls me farther into the shadows that we may observe the goings-on unseen.

Lady Wyckham sweeps past, her footsteps ringing out upon the polished wood floor—*here I am, look at me, watch me*—as she makes her way with much ado to claim a seat beside her monarch, all the time bowing and waving to the assembled throng.

"His Majesty collects fine ladies like he collects spaniels," Lawrence whispers in my ear.

In the center of the great hall is built a stage and around its four sides are the banqueting tables. When all are seated the

King's jester tumbles onto the dais, and the bells on his cap cause the crowd to quiet.

"Your Majesty, the players present for your pleasure tonight a masque entitled *The Honorable Orange Seller!*"

The King rises amidst raucous laughter to hoist a jewel-studded goblet in his right hand. "Let the entertainment commence."

A drummer sets up a throbbing drumbeat, and pipe music floats sweetly into the rafters as an actor dressed in skirts, petticoats, and a bright red wig swaggers upon the stage with a tray about his neck. A chorus of performers cavort about singing of oranges for sale.

"He impersonates Nell Gwyn," murmurs Lawrence. "She is another favorite of the King. Lady Wyckham will be ill-pleased."

I can scarce follow the skit, though it greatly amuses the audience. When the masque is done and the player clapped, servants stagger from the kitchens with food-laden platters. Never have I seen such an array of provender. Lawrence selects samples for me as they pass by so that I can better hold on to pup. Raisins, olives, figs, and such delights as I have never before seen, let alone dreamed, of tasting. We sit upon the floor, our backs to a tapestry covered wall, and devour the treats.

"This is a Nelly orange," says Lawrence, biting into the skin and peeling off a thick rind. He offers me a section, and the juice is wondrous sweet upon my tongue.

Before long, the banquet tables are strewn with chunks of beef and venison, bowls of marigold and spinach mixed with mint, and platters of blackbird, lark, and sparrow, the latter I cannot bear to look upon. But to my dismay they are soon gobbled down by the greedy guests, bones and all.

So lulled am I by the exotic aromas and the rich fodder resting in my belly that my body relaxes. In an instant pup squirms free of my shawl, for she is sore tempted by crusts and crumbs and morsels of meat littering the floor. She dashes about the hall, dodging spills and slops, before darting beneath the King's table.

I dive after her into a forest of stockinged legs, thigh-high boots, and silver shoes. Lawrence calls my name, but I am determined to catch pup. Before I can grab the little minx, however, she spies a bare foot peeking from a silk gown and begins to nip and lick at the lily white toes with gusto.

"Good Sire," squeals the owner of the bare foot, "'tis early in the evening for such games!"

"Indeed it is, good wench," the King responds. "I fear you are much mistaken if you take some attention to be mine."

I grab pup and try to crawl away unheeded, but the monarch's eyes are sharp. "So, little maid Riston, was that my dog annoying Lady Wyckham yet again?" He roars with laughter.

"Yes, Your Majesty," I mutter, dipping to the ground. The animal snuggles into my arms. "I beg your pardon."

"The dog is cured, then?"

"Yes, Sire."

"No more farting?"

"No, Sire."

"Well done, maid." The King claps his hands. "You must instruct my Master of the Kennels. For does seem he has much to learn."

Meanwhile poor Lady Wyckham struggles to find her slipper, and there is a mighty blush upon her cheeks, well matching the circles of rouge daubed atop her white-powdered skin.

"You, Lady Wyckham, what shall I do with the pup?" bellows the King.

But Lady Wyckham has lost her sass. "'Tis your choice, Sire," she murmurs.

"What say you, Madam? I hear you not!"

Lady Wyckham shrugs her powdered shoulders. "I say 'tis your choice, Sire."

"It is indeed," replies the King. "You learn well."

He leans over the table and gazes at me for a long moment. "Take the dog," he says, with a wave of his lace-cuffed hand. "You have earned her. She is yours."

"Thank you, Sire." I sink into another deep curtsey, hardly able to believe my good fortune. "Dearest pup," I murmur, burying my nose in her sweet fur. "Soon you will breathe God's fresh air and scamper upon his wolds."

"Well done, angel here on earth girl," says Pappy, appearing suddenly at my side and drawing me away from the King's table. "Proud I am of you. But I believed all along that you could cure the creature."

"Now, I wish for more amusement," declares King Charles. "Earn you keep, Jester. What shall we play this evening?"

Jester springs upon his hands across the stage. "Queen for a Day, Sire?"

"Indeed," shouts the King. "A splendid choice. Let the music play!"

Once again there is a swirl of pipes and drums, and the troupe of actors bound back into the hall, their arms filled with fresh-gathered mistletoe, which they proceed to weave into a gleaming crown dotted with white waxy berries.

> *Here we go gathering mistletoe,*
> *Mistletoe, mistletoe,*
> *Here we go gathering mistletoe,*
> *On a cold and frosty morning.*

Jester capers in a frenzy, tumbling head over heels, hands over feet, urging one and all into a big circle. Pappy plucks pup from my arms. "Dance, Gwen-child," he says, "for you have earned it well."

I search the hall in vain for sight of Lawrence, but Lady Bathurst clasps her slender hand round mine and draws me into the glittering circle of courtiers. Where can Lawrence have gone? Does seem he has vanished into thin air.

King Charles and his gentlemen skip to the center of the ring. With hands upon their waists, the King's dandies dance a dainty jig before us, all the time singing lustily,

> *Who will be our queen for a day?*
> *Queen for a day, queen for a day?*
> *Who will be our queen for a day?*
> *On a cold and frosty morning.*

Who indeed, I wonder, as we curtsey to the gentlemen. Will His Majesty insist on chosing Lady Wyckham over his sad sovereign queen? Jester swirls about us all holding the gleaming crown of mistletoe above his head. Then we switch about, the courtiers form the outer circle, we ladies the inner, and the gentlemen sing on, louder and louder,

Who will we choose to fetch away?
Fetch away, fetch away?
Who will we choose to fetch away?
On a cold and frosty morning?

Now Jester sets down the crown upon the stage and weaves in and out of the dancers curling a crimson sash above our heads, between our toes. His belled cap twinkles in the dusky flame light. "Who will we chose to fetch away?" he croons.

"Perchance the maid with silver white curls?" shouts King Charles.

"Mayhap the lass with moon-kissed skin?" bellows Lord Bathurst.

Me! I can scarce believe it. But I am thrust before Jester. He ties the sash about my eyes and twirls me once. He twirls me twice. And he twirls me thrice. Round and round until I am so dizzy I can barely keep to my feet.

Who shall we send to fetch her away?
Fetch her away, fetch her away?
Who shall we send to fetch her away?
On a cold and frosty morning.

Chapter Twenty-One

Then all at once I smell the sweetness of a Nelly orange close by my cheek.

> *Lordling Lawrence will fetch her away,*
> *Fetch her away, fetch her away,*
> *Lordling Lawrence will fetch her away,*
> *On a cold and frosty morning.*

I pull the sash from my eyes. Lawrence stands before me, blushing pink, smiling sweet, come to fetch me away. He loops his arm around my waist and dances me about the great hall before the mass of clapping, cheering dandies. My slippers sparkle in the yellow candle glow.

When we are quite without breath, Lawrence escorts me to the gilded throne. Jester swoops forward to place the circlet of greens upon my head. The leaves bristle with the brisk, biting chill of the cold outdoors.

"I declare this special fair maid to be queen for a day," Jester whoops.

In front of the King and all his guests, Lawrence takes my hand. He leans close. So close I smell again the sweet juice of the Nelly orange.

"Forever and a day?" he whispers.

I smile. I am not a witch. I am a healer.

And best of all I am fetched away!

The leaden weight in my chest melts fast as butter on a summer's day. In its place blooms a bright, bold, born-again heart.

author's *note*

When Gwendoline was born, England was a sparsely populated country of about five million people, most of whom lived by growing crops or raising sheep and cattle and rarely left their immediate surroundings. Roads were unpaved. Goods were carried by carts or transported by barges. For ordinary people dirt, flies, fleas, and lice were a normal part of life. As were rats! People did not know about germs and hardly ever washed. One baby in three died before reaching the age of five.

Shortly before Gwendoline was born her country suffered its only civil war, fought between supporters of King Charles I and Parliament troops led by Oliver Cromwell. The Parliament troops won in 1645, and Oliver Cromwell became Lord Protector of England. A staunch Puritan, he banned many ordinary

pastimes like games and dancing and feasts. Eighteen months
after Cromwell's death, Parliament invited the exiled king back
to England. In 1660 King Charles II regained his throne bringing his easy going ways. He loved to sing and dance, as he does
in this story. Although it is true that the King sought shelter in
Oxford, it is pure make-believe that during his visit a young
girl healed one of his dogs!

In Gwendoline's day people truly believed that witches lived
among them, and women with a knowledge of herbs and a
gift of healing were often a target. As long as they were able to
cure illness or successfully deliver babies these women were
safe—but if a baby died or livestock sickened or, God forbid, a
catastrophe like the plague struck, they were doomed. The last
execution for witchcraft in England did not take place until
1712—when Gwendoline would have been sixty-one years old.

When the Great Plague reached Letchlade, Gwendoline
observed that the villagers died in different ways. We now know
that the plague is a bacterial disease infecting the blood of rats
and transferred to humans by fleas, and we identify the plague
in three separate categories:

Bubonic Plague is an infection of the lymphatic system.
Symptoms include chills, fever, and delirium, followed by
swollen lymph nodes called buboes. Most victims die within
ten days.

Pneumonic Plague is either a secondary spread of the initial
bubonic form to the lungs or transmitted from human to human.
Symptoms include bloody coughing, fever, headache, weakness,

chest pain, coma, and death. This category is much more con-tagious because the bacteria can be passed into the air through coughing and infect any passerby who inhales that germ.

Septicemic Plague results when bacteria enters the blood from the lymphatic and respiratory systems, respectively. A rash develops and death occurs within twenty-four hours.

Gwendoline noticed too that some of the villagers did not get sick. It is now believed that some lucky people carry a natural immunity to the plague, passed down through ancestors who contracted but survived the plague hundreds of years ago. And since the discovery of antibiotics, outbreaks of the bubonic plague in Europe and the US are rare.

the *glossary*

Beaker   A large drinking bowl or cup.

Bedlam   The Hospital of St. Mary of Bethlehem, an institu-
                    tion in London for the mentally ill.

Buboes   Inflamed, tender swellings of lymph nodes in
                    armpits and groins, characteristic of infections
                    such as the plague.

Cavalier/   A dashing officer and supporter of King Charles I
Royalist   during the English Civil War.

Civil War   Disagreement between King Charles I and
1642–1645   Parliament, which escalated into war. Oliver
                    Cromwell, a Puritan country gentleman, organized
                    Parliament's army into a well-trained force. Many
                    saw it as a holy war, a battle for freedom of religion,
                    and at the Battle of Naseby in 1645 the King's

Royalists were utterly defeated. King Charles I was beheaded in 1649 and Parliament proclaimed that England would henceforth be a Commonwealth. Cromwell became Lord Protector. The Commonwealth continued until the Restoration.

Cromwell, Oliver

Defeated King Charles I in England's only Civil War (1642–1645). He was Lord Protector until his death in 1658 and ruled the land with an iron fist. All games, dances, and feasts were banned and the people were forced to wear plain, dull clothing.

Dray

Low heavy cart without sides, used for hauling.

Flagon

A pottery vessel for holding ale or wine.

Fortnight

Two weeks.

Plague

The plague first appeared in Europe in the mid-fourteenth century. The plague was carried by fleas that lived on rats. If an infected rat flea bit a human being, he or she became infected. There was no known cure and few people survived. In the Great Plague of 1665 about 100,000 people died in England. Hundreds of people left London in an attempt to escape the disease.

❧ Glossary ❦

Poupen   Defecation. From Middle English, to break wind.

Puritan   One aiming at greater strictness in religious life and purity of worship.

Quack   A person making fraudulent claims of medical skills and knowledge.

Restoration   In 1660 Charles II (son of Charles I) was restored to the throne. His reign is referred to as the Restoration.

Roundhead   A Puritan, so called in the time of Charles I, for having hair cut close to the head.

Settle   A long high-backed bench.

Smithy   The workshop of a smith, one who forges and shapes iron with an anvil and hammer. One who makes repairs and fits horseshoes.

Spelk   Long thin slivers of wood used for lighting candles from burning embers.

Spindle-whorl   The spindle tree draws its name from the age long use of its thin stems as spindles for the hand spinning of wool. Before the spinning wheel was invented, all woolen thread needed for cloth was spun by hand, usually by women (known as spinsters) who twirled short sticks in one hand. One end of the stick carried a thick hollow disc of stone or metal—the spindle-whorl —which maintained a steady momentum. With the other hand the spinner fed in loosely twisted wool from a hank, and the spindle drew it out into tight thread.

Spinney A small stand or grove of trees.

Swingle-tree A stick, part of the harness attached beneath a horse's tail.

Teazel A plant with large burrs or heads covered with stiff hooked awns, used in raising a nap or cloth.

Vestry A small room adjoining a church in which vestments (ritual robes worn to celebrate mass) are kept.

Wheelwright One who builds and repairs wheels.

Wolds An open track of low rolling hills.